Oliver
Cromwell

The Most
Hated Man
in Irish History

Also by Rod Smith

Get Out and Play GAA
Get Out and Play Football
Get Out and Play Rugby

From the *In a Nutshell (Heroes)* Series:
Pádraig Pearse and the Easter Rising 1916
James Connolly – Working Class Hero
Michael Collins – The Big Fellow
Éamon de Valera – Dev
Charles Stewart Parnell – The Uncrowned King
of Ireland

From the *In a Nutshell (Myths and Legends)* Series:
Saint Colmcille (Saint Columba)

Published by Poolbeg Press

Oliver
Cromwell

The Most
Hated Man
in Irish History

Liam and Aoife's Story

ROD SMITH

Published 2018
by Poolbeg Press Ltd
123 Grange Hill, Baldoyle
Dublin 13, Ireland
E-mail: poolbeg@poolbeg.com

© ROD SMITH 2018

The moral right of the author has been asserted.

Typesetting, editing, layout, design, ebook © Poolbeg Press Ltd.

1

 record for this book is available from the British Library.

ISBN 978-1-78199-848-9

Typeset by Poolbeg Press Ltd

Cover illustrated by Derry Dillon

Printed by CPI Group, UK

www.poolbeg.com

About the Author

Rod Smith was born in Drogheda. He lives in Malahide with his wife Denise and sons Alex and Oisín. This is his tenth book, and his first historical novel. He is a graduate of Dublin City University where he holds a Bachelor of Arts and a Master's Degree. He is currently studying for a Master's in Creative Writing at the Open University.

Dedication

For Denise, Alex, Oisín, my mother Betty, and in memory of dear Jennie

Preface

Oliver Cromwell was born on the 25th April 1599 in Huntingdon, Cambridgeshire, England. He was a radical Puritan who became a Member of Parliament in the House of Commons in 1628. He joined the English Parliamentary Army in 1643 as a cavalry captain and despite a lack of military experience rose to become commander-in-chief of the army by 1650. He also helped to form a well-disciplined and organised army called the New Model Army which defeated the forces of King Charles I in the two English Civil Wars.

After the king was executed in 1649, Cromwell led an army to fight in Ireland against an alliance of Irish Confederate Catholics and English Royalists. After leaving Ireland, he defeated the Scottish armies who supported Charles II's claim to the throne. He dissolved Parliament and became Lord Protector of England, Ireland, Scotland and Wales in 1653.

After his death in 1658 at the age of 59, his son Richard succeeded him. However, he soon was forced to resign, and Parliament was restored. By 1660, Charles II was returned to the throne. Cromwell's body was removed from its burial place at Westminster Abbey, hung and then beheaded.

Although voted the tenth greatest Briton in British history in a BBC poll in 2002, Cromwell has proved to be a very divisive figure in history, with some people viewing him as a hero and others as a villain.

This book focuses on Cromwell's time in Ireland and tries to show the huge impact he had on the island and its people in such a short period of time. The author has done his utmost to ensure that, whenever possible, all of the historical events in this book are based on sound historical evidence. However, some artistic licence has been used in the aims of furthering the story and keeping the interest of the younger reader.

While this book provides only a snapshot of the life of Cromwell, perhaps it will encourage you to find out more about this individual, and ultimately help you to come to your own conclusions as you try to separate the man from the myth.

"Paint my picture truly like me, and flatter me not at all; but remark all these roughness, pimples, warts and everything as you see me. Otherwise I will never pay a farthing for it."
Oliver Cromwell to his portrait painter

"Cromwell was about 50% saint and about 50% serpent."
Professor Ronald Hutton, Professor of History, Bristol University

"The English did terrible things in Ireland in 1649 and the 1650s, and it is wrong to blame Cromwell for all of them — that lets other Englishmen much more to blame than him off the hook."
John Morrill HonMRIA, Emeritus Professor of British and Irish History, University of Cambridge

Chapter 1

The School Trip

Stop right there! Listen to me. My name is Liam O'Malley and I am nearly twelve years old. I have to warn you. What follows is a tale that is exciting, terrifying and unbelievable! If you feel brave enough to continue, then I salute your courage. Don't say you weren't told . . .

Do you think history is boring? I used to. All those facts and figures! Enough to put you to sleep! I'd rather be using my smartphone! However, I have a story to tell that you will not believe – but I promise it's true. I hope you believe me!

It started on a typical school day. Well, not typical.

For once I was looking forward to going to school! We were going on a school trip and anything that would get me out of that building was a welcome relief.

My mum dropped me to the bus and got out to say goodbye.

I was surprised at that. Usually she just dropped me and headed off with a wave as soon as I got out.

"Liam, can the baby and I give you a hug before you head off or are you too old for that now?" she asked.

"Oh Mum, the baby isn't born yet!"

"It's coming any day now! And I know it wants a hug before you go!"

I threw my arms around her. "I can hardly get my arms around you with your big tummy!" I said with a laugh.

We hugged for a moment.

"I don't want to let you go!" she said.

"Mum! What's the matter with you? I'm not going to Australia or up the Amazon! It's just a day trip!"

"I know. I hope you have a great time! I'll see you later. Stay safe! The baby is waving goodbye – I can feel it!"

"Oh, Mum!"

"You won't be an only child for much longer!"

"*Come on now, class, hurry up! We don't want to be late!*" bellowed Mr Clarke, the class teacher. "*The bus won't wait, you know!*"

We all queued up to take our places on the bus. I looked back one more time to find that Mum was still standing there watching me. Much later I was to wonder if she had a premonition of what was to come.

"Another boring school trip!" groaned my friend Mikhail as he swung his wheelchair in beside me and waited in line to get on the bus.

"Tell me about it!" agreed Nuala. "I'm missing a school basketball training session for this!"

"Are you serious?" I replied. "We're going on a bus, on the open road. This has to count as a day off school!"

When we had taken our seats, Mr Clarke stood up at the front of the bus to address us. He was a medium-sized man, with a brown beard and piercing brown eyes hidden behind a pair of spectacles with dark-blue frames. He had one continuous eyebrow that looked like a caterpillar living in solitude above his eyes.

"Now, class, I have some exciting news for you. This is no ordinary school trip. This is an Extra-Special Surprise School Trip!"

"I don't like the sound of *an extra-special surprise*!" groaned Mikhail.

"Now, now, class, settle down," Mr Clarke continued. "Do you remember the school project you all did on Oliver Cromwell?"

I looked around at the others. Everyone kept their heads down and pretended not to hear in case they were asked a question.

"The school project you all spent weeks working on? Anyone? Can anyone remember anything about Cromwell?"

Mr Rafferty the bus driver, who had been silent up until now, spoke up.

"The most hated man in Irish history – everyone knows about the Curse of Cromwell," he said ominously.

"Well done, Mr Rafferty! The Curse of Cromwell indeed! Anyone else?"

Suddenly lots of hands shot up around the bus.

"If he could do curses was he a wizard, sir?"

"No!"

"Or was he known for using bad language, sir?" I asked.

"No, he was not, O'Malley! Right, that's enough! As you all *should* know, Oliver Cromwell came to Ireland with an army in 1649."

"Weren't his soldiers called Roundheads?" Sanjay asked. "Because mostly they had their hair cut short and long hair was the fashion at the time?"

"That's right, Sanjay!" Mr Clarke looked amazed and thrilled that someone had remembered *something*. But that didn't last long.

8

"Is he still alive, sir, and walks the earth as a zombie? Is that why there's a curse?" Pat O'Brien asked.

"No, he is *not* still alive, O'Brien, and he is *not* a zombie!"

"Well, technically zombies aren't alive anyway, sir," said Pat. "He would be undead if he was a zombie."

"Did he like to eat people, sir?" Mikhail asked. "Zombies like to eat people!"

Mr Clarke buried his head in his hands.

"Let's go, Rafferty. I don't think I can take much more of this," I heard him whisper.

Mr Rafferty started the engine and the bus pulled away from the school.

"But where are we going, sir?" I asked.

"To Drogheda, where Cromwell and his army besieged the town."

"What is the extra-special surprise, sir?" Nuala asked.

"Oh yes, the surprise! You are all going to take part in a re-enactment of the Siege of Drogheda! Isn't that exciting?"

I threw my eyes up to heaven. Nobody on the bus spoke.

"Well, I think it's exciting," Mr Clarke muttered to himself.

"You had better sit down, Mr Clarke," Mr Rafferty

said. "We're about to head onto the motorway, so we'll be travelling quite fast,"

"I'll be fine," he said as *"Bump!"* the bus seemed to hit something, and he was thrown to the ground.

"Are you all right, sir?" asked Sanjay who was sitting up front.

Mr Clarke picked himself up off the floor and brushed himself down.

"I hope that wasn't the Curse of Cromwell coming to you, Mr Clarke!" I joked.

"I wouldn't be surprised," Mr Rafferty muttered. "I *told* him to sit down."

Mr Clarke sat down and remained silent for the rest of the journey.

At last we arrived at a large field which was packed full of people dressed up in old costumes and armour. On a high mound to the left, pointing down onto the field, there were a couple of real-looking cannons on wheels.

"Who are those people, sir?" I asked.

"They are the historical re-enactment group. You will be working with them today."

My eyes nearly popped out of my head when I looked around and saw piles of smaller armour, clothes and weapons on a long wooden table.

"Do we get to wear that armour, sir?" I asked.

"Yes, you do!"

"When, sir?"

"Right now, O'Malley!"

"When do we get to hold the weapons, sir?" Mikhail asked.

"As soon as you have the armour on!"

"When do we get lunch, sir?" Pat asked.

"As soon as you let Cromwell win the battle," Mr Clarke sighed.

"Will that take long, sir?"

"In your case, I shouldn't think so!" Mr Clarke said with a laugh.

"I can't wait!" Nuala said sarcastically. "Just what I don't need – boys with their big toys!"

We were greeted by a group of enthusiastic volunteers who dressed us up in the type of clothing and armour worn at the time. They also gave us swords – wooden, of course!

"You will be members of the Drogheda garrison under Commander Aston!" Mr Clarke shouted, now looking excited. "And you'll be fighting against Cromwell's soldiers as they try to overcome Drogheda! You'll be the Royalist soldiers!"

"Does that mean we'll be treated like a king, sir?" I asked.

"No, O'Malley. It means you support the king."

"But isn't he dead, sir? Didn't Cromwell kill him?" Mikhail asked.

"That's right, they chopped his head off!" Pat shouted.

Mr Clarke shook his head. "That was Charles the First. His son, Charles the Second, is the king now, except he is not recognised as the king because England is now a commonwealth. Why was it called a commonwealth, class?"

Silence reigned.

Mr Clarke sighed.

"Because all the common people were wealthy!" chanced Pat.

"Not a bad guess, O'Brien, not bad," said Mr Clarke. "It means a country founded for the common good of the people."

"Who are you dressed as, sir?" Sanjay asked as Mr Clarke started to put on an impressive military costume.

"I'm Commander Aston, of course! Commander of the Royalist forces in Drogheda – also its governor. I will be leading you all in this glorious fight against Cromwell and his New Model Army!"

"Did they like building models, sir?" Pat asked, just to annoy Mr Clarke.

Mr Clarke sighed and shook his head. He was handed a fake wooden leg to put over his own leg. He cheered up immediately.

"Of course! Aston had a wooden leg!" he said excitedly.

We were all led to the middle of the field where we were given our instructions by Mr Clarke.

"Now, class, there are twenty-five of us in total. Twelve of you will remain here. Cromwell's soldiers are going to appear over there, through the big gap in that fake wall, which is supposed to be the city wall breached by cannon fire. You are going to try and fight them back. The other twelve will join me. I will be commanding everything from up on that hill which is supposed to be Millmount Fort."

Mr Clarke separated us into two groups. Twelve, including Pat, Nuala and me, took up places facing the fake breached wall. The others went with Mr Clarke.

We stood there, quite excited now, waiting for the enemy troops to come pouring through the breach.

"*I'm ready for battle!*" Pat shouted as he waved his sword. "*Bring 'em on! Avast, ye landlubbers!*"

"That's pirate talk!" I laughed.

"Why is Mr Rafferty running towards us?" Nuala asked suddenly as she looked back across the field.

"What's he saying?" said Pat.

"I think he's saying '*cannon*'," Nuala said. "What does he mean?"

Now Mr Rafferty was pointing, and I looked to our left to see a runaway cannon coming at us at full speed.

13

"Look out!" I shouted as I pushed Pat and Nuala out of the way.

I felt somebody grab me ... then a shattering blow to my head and everything went dark . . .

Chapter 2

Drogheda, 1649

I heard lots of shouts and screaming. A voice in the distance was calling me. A girl's voice.

"Wake up, Liam, wake up!"

I opened my eyes slowly and blinked them a couple of times to try and clear my vision, but it remained blurred.

"Please get up, Liam, or it will be too late!"

"Too late for the bus?" I mumbled.

"Bus? What do you mean?" came a male voice. "Come on, Liam, get up or you may be killed where you lie!"

Sight came back to me and I saw lots of bodies in military uniform lying around. I realised I was still wearing the battle costume I had been fitted with.

"Wow, this re-enactment is very realistic!" I said.

But I didn't recognise the place. Where was the field? I was lying on rubble and around me were streets and high walls.

Suddenly a strong pair of arms lifted me to my feet.

"What's wrong with him?" asked the male voice.

"I think he took a bang to the head, sir," said the girl.

"Well, get him away from here if you can – this is no place for children. The walls are breached here in two places – on either side of the church – it's only a matter of time before they get in. Go to Millmount Fort. Commander Aston is there. He may have some new orders for you."

"Yes, Captain Kelly. Come on, Liam."

A brown-haired girl, who looked about my age, gently took my hand. She was wearing a dirty blue dress and grey stockings.

"You're all right now, Liam. My name's Aoife. I'm here to help."

I still felt dazed. "Are we going back to the bus?"

"What is this mysterious bus you speak about?"

"The bus to take us home."

"Home? Don't worry, Liam – I promise I will protect you and get you back there safely."

"You? But where's the bus? Where are the others?" I held my head which felt very sore.

Suddenly there was a shout in the distance.

"They have made it into the town! Retreat! Retreat!"

Then a different voice could be heard, full of menace. *"Aston refused to surrender peacefully yesterday when I gave him the opportunity. He will now pay the price. No quarter to anyone bearing arms! No quarter to be given! Kill anyone with a weapon!"*

A group of men ran past us, towards the commotion.

"To the southern breach, men!" shouted their leader. *"We must save the town!"*

"Come on, Liam! We have to get to Millmount!" Aoife cried, sounding convincingly frightened.

She must be one of the re-enactment group, I realised – though I hadn't seen any children among them earlier.

"But I really don't feel good, Aoife – my head is spinning. There must be some First Aid people around in case of accidents – can't you take me to them?"

"Run!" she yelled.

I stood there, confused, my head throbbing with pain.

"Run, please!" she screamed as she grabbed my hand.

I had no choice but to run with her as the shouts and screams grew closer.

We ran through the streets until we came to Millmount Fort. It was at the top of a large grassy mound.

It was guarded by a nervous-looking group of soldiers. One of them approached us.

"What are you doing here? State your business?"

"Please, sir, we were asked to report to Commander Aston to receive fresh orders," Aoife panted. "Cromwell himself is down there with his troops. They are killing everyone who stands in their way."

The soldier's face went white.

"Come this way," he said. "I'll take you to the commander directly."

We were taken to the main dining room where some officers were looking over a series of maps on a large table.

The soldier left us to return to his post.

A tall man with an English accent and a wooden leg was leading the discussion.

"Commander Aston, Cromwell and his troops are in the town!" I blurted out without thinking.

"Thank you, boy. They breached the walls yesterday. Cromwell is obviously angry that we did not accept his offer of surrender. We were hoping that reinforcements would arrive, but this is not going to happen now. He will send some of his best soldiers here to find us. If anyone wishes to leave, now is the time to do so."

Everyone remained.

Commander Aston saluted the group. "Thank you, gentlemen."

Then he hobbled over to us.

"Brave children, thank you for this message. You should go now before the soldiers arrive."

"Have you any new orders for us, sir?" Aoife asked.

"Save yourselves," he replied. "We will need courageous people once this battle is over. If the town falls, make your way to Wexford." He then went and sat at the table. Pulling paper, pen and ink towards him, he began to write a letter. A minute later he rose and handed the folded letter to me. "This is a letter addressed to Colonel Sinnott in Wexford, telling him what has happened here. I have sent other messengers to some of the towns. However, as you are children you might be able to get through where my own messengers may not, as you should be above suspicion. Now find yourself a safe place to hide until all this is over."

I nodded and put the letter inside my shirt, not too happy about it. This re-enactment was fantastic, but I wasn't feeling well and I'd had enough.

"They are on the streets below!" a voice from outside shouted. It was the soldier who had brought us in. *"They are coming this way! Colonel Axtell is at the bottom of the mound. He is offering us the opportunity to surrender."*

"Commander, they will not let you surrender!" Aoife exclaimed. "They are killing everyone. We heard a voice order that no quarter be given!"

"If it saves the lives of the soldiers here with me, I have no choice but to accept the offer. Go quickly now, children. There is a gate at the back you can escape through. I will give the order to my men to surrender."

Outside the room I stopped. "Aoife," I said, "this is all great but, please, can't we –"

"*Come on!*" Aoife grabbed my hand and dragged me with her.

We ran to the gate which was deserted and ajar. We darted out and down Millmount Fort hill. We ran on and crossed the drawbridge over the River Boyne which, Aoife said, separated the north from the south of the town.

By this time Cromwell's soldiers were flooding the streets and killing anyone they met. I saw a priest being clubbed on the head with a rock by some soldiers. He fell to the ground and did not move. Ordinary civilians who were not armed were also being killed as the soldiers rampaged through the town. There was blood everywhere.

Suddenly I realised with a sickening feeling that it was all real. People were actually dying around us. I didn't understand how it could be so – but it was.

"We need a safe place to hide," Aoife whispered. "Maybe St Peter's Church? They will not dare to enter a church that offers sanctuary."

"How far is it?"

She pointed. "Up the hill straight ahead, at the top of St Peter's Street."

We ran towards it and darted in. Others had the same idea. People rushed in the doors, fleeing from the battle. They hid up in the wooden steeple. Some were crying, some were shouting while others were praying.

"No, we must leave!" I suddenly gasped. "Something doesn't feel right!"

"Why? It's a church!" said Aoife.

"It's not safe. We need to get away from here."

As I looked behind I could see a large number of Cromwell's soldiers running towards the church, continuing to kill everyone and everything that stood in their way. It was too late to leave by the main door. We ran and hid behind a big carved wooden partition.

Cromwell's soldiers entered the church and began killing people. The screaming was terrible. We trembled in fear. When the soldiers realised that people were hiding in the steeple, they gathered together the wooden pews and piled them up at its base. Then they set fire to them.

"They're burning the people in the steeple!" Aoife whispered in terror.

"And next they'll come to take this wooden partition to burn!" I said. "We must get out of here!"

At risk of our lives, we raced past some soldiers to the door and out onto the street. This time it was my turn to grab Aoife's hand and run into the safety of darkness. No one followed us.

We hid at a safe distance from the church in a barn where we listened in horror as people were burned alive.

"*Oh God, I burn! I burn!*" came a shout amidst all of the screams.

"Those poor people!" I sobbed.

Suddenly a dishevelled soldier ran into the barn and threw himself down on the hay. He lay there moaning in pain. He had been stabbed in the chest and was bleeding profusely.

His face looked familiar. It was the soldier from the battlefield earlier in the day.

Aoife went rushing over to him. She tore off part of her underskirt and used it as a bandage to try to stop the bleeding.

"Captain Kelly! What happened to you?"

"Aoife, you're all right!" He tried to smile despite the obvious pain. "And your friend, where is he?"

"I'm right here, sir – I'm fine!"

"Brave children!" he moaned as his breathing grew shallower.

"Is there anything we can do to help?" I asked.

"I am done for. You must get out to safety. You can't go to the north. Dundalk is going to surrender without a fight, and Cromwell's allies are marching through the northern counties."

"Commander Aston asked us to go to Wexford to warn them there."

"Aston is dead," Captain Kelly whispered.

"Dead? But he surrendered peacefully and was promised safe quarter for himself and his men!" I protested.

"He and his men were taken to a nearby windmill and killed. They beat Aston to death with his own wooden leg. The soldiers thought there might be gold coins hidden in the leg."

"*Savage brutes!*" Aoife cried.

A loud whinnying noise came from outside. A saddled and bridled chestnut-brown horse walked through the barn door, approached the captain and nuzzled his face.

"Ferdia!" the captain groaned, raising a hand to stroke the horse's face. "I left him at Mary Street in safety, but he has followed me here."

The horse looked at each of us for a moment as if sizing us up, and then turned back to look at its master.

"Wexford is hundreds of miles away," said the captain. "It's lucky Ferdia did follow me – he will lead you to safety and help you to get there."

Meanwhile Ferdia started to eat some of the hay the captain was lying on.

"That horse is always hungry!" the captain joked, despite the pain.

"What about you, captain?" I asked.

"I don't have the strength to get back on the horse. I am done for."

"Well, we're not leaving you here to die!" Aoife declared.

"No way!" I agreed.

We both tried to lift the captain up, but he was too heavy for us. He was too badly hurt to provide much help.

Suddenly there was the sound of a group of soldiers outside and they were in the barn before we knew it.

Aoife and I stood in front of the injured captain to hide him from their gaze.

"What's all this?" said a voice in the midst of the group.

All of the soldiers drew back as a dark figure, with a hooked nose and shoulder-length hair, and a large wart between his mouth and chin strode purposefully towards us.

"Cromwell!" I gasped.

Cromwell stared at me with quizzical eyes.

"You know me, boy?"

"I have heard stories about you ... sir," I mumbled nervously.

"Have you indeed? Well, don't believe everything you hear, boy. What's this you're trying so hard to hide?"

Two of his soldiers grabbed us and threw us roughly to the ground. They took out their swords and stood over us.

"*Wait!*" Cromwell shouted. He drew his sword as well.

I thought that this was going to be the end of us.

Instead he pointed the weapon at the two soldiers who had roughly manhandled us.

"*We are not here to kill civilians in cold blood. Do not harm these children!*" he roared.

The soldiers shrank back in fear as Cromwell himself helped us to our feet. It was then that he noticed the injured captain in the straw.

"So, this is what you were trying to hide," he said mockingly. "I salute your bravery but disapprove of your foolish action."

Captain Kelly stared up at Cromwell defiantly.

"Shall we kill him, sir?" one of the soldiers asked.

"These children have risked their lives to protect him. I too have children. I see God's light in their faces. Perhaps it is God's will that this renegade should live to see the morrow. Who am I to go against the will of God? Leave them be."

Aoife gasped.

I couldn't believe it. "Thank you, general," I managed to say.

"Do not thank me, boy. I have stepped over many

dead bodies of officers and soldiers who have served me faithfully. They have met their end here due to the refusal of this town to surrender. There will be no mercy shown and no quarter given. This is a righteous judgement of God upon these barbarous wretches who took the lives of my Protestant brethren, including many women and children like yourselves, in the 1641 Irish rebellion. They all have blood on their hands, particularly your Catholic priests and monks."

"You shouldn't believe all of the stories you've heard about 1641," I replied as one of Mr Clarke history lessons sprang into my mind.

"Liam, what are you doing?" Aoife whispered.

"Many of those stories about atrocities committed on the Protestants are not true. They were exaggerated so you would have an excuse to invade Ireland!" The words were out of my mouth before I realised how dangerous they were.

Cromwell looked at me in silence. I could feel his gaze pierce into my very soul.

"Why do you hate the Irish so?" Aoife asked Cromwell, and I knew she was trying to distract his attention from me.

"I have no particular fondness for the Irish, girl," he replied, "but I do not hate them. The Irish are too willing and eager to follow the words of their foolish priests and this does not do them any favours.

Besides, many of the soldiers who have fallen to our swords today are English Royalists who want a king again."

"Charles the Second! Whose father you beheaded!" I said boldly, and Aoife glared at me.

"Choose your next words wisely, boy. It was not murder, but the will of God and his people."

One of the other soldiers broke the silence.

"What about the horse, sir?" he said, pointing at Ferdia.

"Horse?" Cromwell asked, as his mind snapped back to the present.

"That's my horse!" I lied.

"Would you steal from a child?" Cromwell barked at the soldier.

And with that he strode to the door of the barn, followed by his men.

"Leave this town," he said as he turned to face us one more time. "What is happening in this town is not for the eyes of children. What we do tonight will send a message to other towns that dare to defy us. If you fight us, there will be an effusion of blood."

Then he and his men were gone.

Aoife and I looked at one another.

"Why did you speak to him like that?" she asked angrily. "He could have killed you."

She was right, of course, and now that it was over

my knees were knocking a bit.

The groans of the captain brought us back to our senses. We found the strength to get him up off the ground and put him standing beside Ferdia.

"There's a mounting block on the street," he gasped.

With the captain using the horse for support, we set off down the street. Soldiers passed us by but no one touched or threatened us. Maybe word had gone out that we were not to be harmed.

We soon came across a stone mounting block at the side of the street and Captain Kelly managed to mount Ferdia.

We picked up our pace then and soon arrived at the gates of the town. There were no soldiers on guard there and we walked out into the countryside.

"Don't look back," I said to Aoife.

We continued for about a mile and then we came upon a group of six nuns who had fled the town beforehand. We told them what we had witnessed in the town and they were horrified to hear of the burning of the church steeple and the slaughter.

"My daughters," said an older nun to the others, "there will be time for grieving and praying later. Now we must seek shelter. And God has delivered these children and a wounded man into our care."

She then offered to take us with them to a secret

location where they had friends who would hide us all from Cromwell's men. We were glad to let them take care of the captain, who was by now very weak from loss of blood and looked deathly pale, but we knew we had to continue on our journey to Wexford.

Captain Kelly slid down from Ferdia's back. "Take Ferdia and go now, children," he said. "You have orders from Commander Aston himself. They must be obeyed."

"We hate to leave you," Aoife said.

"Don't worry, I know where you're going. I will follow as soon as I can. You will need to travel to Dublin first and then onward to Wexford. When you get to Dublin, find my uncle Phelim McCarthy. He works at the docks at Wood Quay, right by the River Liffey. He will be able to find you a ship that is sailing to Wexford. It will save you a long and dangerous journey by land."

The nuns gave us some dry bread and water for the journey and then a sturdy young nun helped Aoife to mount Ferdia and adjusted the stirrups to suit her. She then gave me a leg-up onto Ferdia behind Aoife.

"But we don't know the way to Dublin," I said.

"Don't worry – Ferdia knows the way," said the captain. "We have visited Uncle Phelim many times. He had him when he was just a foal. Once you get to the docks, look for Winetavern Street. He will be in one of the public houses there. Listen out for the man who complains about everything. That will be Phelim."

As if he understood, Ferdia went to where Captain Kelly was sitting on a rock. The captain put his arm around his neck and stroked him gently. Ferdia drew closer to the captain and nuzzled him for one last time.

"God bless and protect you!" the older nun cried as we set off on the path for Dublin.

I was a little nervous – I had never been on a horse before – but clearly Aoife had. She held the reins confidently while I had my arms around her waist.

Ferdia neighed loudly and started to gallop southwards. The next step of our adventure was about to begin!

After a while, as I looked up into the night sky, I saw what looked like a very bright star that dominated all others. I thought my eyes were playing tricks. It seemed to be getting closer to me at a very slow rate.

"Do you see that, Aoife!" I said as I pointed up into the sky.

She pulled on the reins and Ferdia slowed down and halted.

"It's beautiful," she said, staring upwards.

"I wonder what it is?"

"It's home," I thought I heard her whisper.

"What?"

"Never mind."

She drummed her heels into Ferdia's sides and we rode off into the night.

Chapter 3

Dublin, 1649

We travelled through the countryside in darkness. There were no lights to guide us or signs of any people on the way. Everyone was hiding for fear of coming face to face with Cromwell's army. I still felt very confused, but I was not afraid. Ferdia seemed to know the direction he was going, and there was something about Aoife that made me feel safe. Somehow, I felt nothing bad would happen to me if she was with me.

We rode for hours through the night, just stopping for short breaks on the way. Eventually we reached the outskirts of Dublin. The gates to the city were guarded by Cromwell's soldiers but they let us pass through without any hindrance.

It was early morning and the inhabitants of the city

were beginning to wake up. We made our way through the city and once we hit the River Liffey we headed down Merchants Quay. There were lots of small boats on the river and the quays were full of people loading and unloading goods and supplies onto them.

Aoife and I slid off Ferdia and walked alongside him.

"Captain Kelly said Ferdia knows the way," Aoife said.

"I hope so!" I said. "What was the name of that street?"

"Winetavern Street."

"Should we ask?"

"Let's just follow Ferdia."

He certainly seemed to be moving ahead confidently.

At the end of Merchants Quay, where Wood Quay began, Ferdia suddenly turned right into a side street. Halting, he swung his head around to make sure we were following.

"Yes, this is it – Winetavern Street," said Aoife.

"Let's hope we find this Phelim person here," I said.

Ferdia led us on.

As we walked we strained to hear the voices of the people inside each building.

"How are we going to recognise the voice of

someone we have never met before?" I wondered as we made our way down the street.

"Let's just hope Ferdia does!"

Just then we heard a raised voice coming from one of the bakeries nearby.

"You have some nerve to claim that this bread is fresh! What did you put in it – sawdust? This is shameful. My money and I are leaving this establishment and will never darken its door again, unless you replace this immediately!"

Ferdia whinnied, and his ears pricked up as if he had just recognised a familiar voice. Up he walked to the bakery entrance and stuck his head through the door. A shout of surprise came from inside.

"What kind of place is this that allows scraggly horses enter? Get out of here, you old windbag! Can't you see I'm trying to buy breakfast!" the same voice roared.

To our amazement Ferdia walked right into the shop. The shouts from within intensified. Within a few seconds he was pushing out a tall man, with thin greying hair, who was holding a loaf of bread in his hand.

"Can't a man dine in piece without interruption!" he roared at Ferdia.

Then he dropped the bread and gave Ferdia a big hug.

"Good to see you, old boy!" he laughed as he patted the horse on the nose.

"Now that is no ordinary horse!" I said in admiration.

The man heard us and walked over.

"He is certainly not ordinary! He is a very special horse, well-bred and very clever. So, who are these people you have brought, Ferdia?"

Aoife replied first. "I'm Aoife, and this is Liam."

"Nice to meet you. I'm Phelim. Where is my nephew Captain Kelly?"

"We had to leave him with some nuns outside Drogheda because he was wounded. He gave us Ferdia to guide us to you," I explained.

"Don't worry about the captain, Phelim," Aoife said earnestly. "The nuns will nurse him back to health. They took him to a secret hiding place."

We then explained what had happened at the church and barn and our meeting with Cromwell.

"They didn't kill us, imagine!" Aoife said.

"They wanted to, but Cromwell wouldn't let them."

Phelim stroked his stubbly chin. "You don't say."

"Yes, really," I said. "It was decent of him, I guess."

"I don't think that will come as any comfort to the families of all the people his army has killed so far," Phelim said bitterly.

He was right. I frowned. Cromwell's behaviour was really puzzling.

A battalion of soldiers marched by. They were all

wearing red coats and plain metal helmets with a metal peak in front.

Cromwell's soldiers! I froze to the spot, sure they were going to arrest us, but they passed by without paying us any attention.

Phelim spat on the ground after they walked by. "Dublin is full of these New Model Army soldiers, curse them all!"

"Why hasn't there been a battle here?" I asked.

"There was one, before Cromwell set his cursed feet on this island. His supporters won the day, and Dublin now proudly supports Cromwell and his gang of killers."

It was all so complicated. Well, one thing was clear: we had to deliver the letter.

"How can we get to Wexford?" I asked Phelim. "We've been sent by Commander Aston, who is dead now, to warn Colonel Sinnott. Captain Kelly said you might be able to find us a ship?"

"Wexford is it now? Well, come with me down to the docks, and be mindful of who you talk to and what you say. Remember there are many here who support Cromwell and they would be only too happy to have an opportunity to arrest someone who is against him."

We all walked back to Wood Quay. Phelim spoke with a group of rough-looking sailors who were loading barrels into a small boat on the Liffey. He seemed to be arguing with them for a while, then eventually he called us over.

"This is my good friend Seamus. He has a ship sailing to Wexford with supplies this very morning."

"Don't believe everything he says," Seamus replied as he put his hand on his sword. "I'm not his good friend but I am sailing to Wexford today."

I looked at the tiny boat they were loading the supplies onto. "That's a very small boat you have," I said.

Both Phelim and Seamus burst into laughter.

"The waters here are too shallow for ships," Seamus explained. "That's only our little 'lighter' that we use for transporting goods from the ship to the docks."

Another group of Cromwell's soldiers arrived at the dock. They started to question some of the people who were unloading supplies. One of the soldiers looked over at us and kept staring at us.

"Come on now, you'd best be moving – we're starting to draw some unwanted attention," Phelim muttered.

"For once you're right, Phelim," said Seamus. "Come on now, children, pick up those bags of flour there and come with me.'

"I'll go with you," Phelim replied. "I can row the lighter back when you're finished with it."

"What about Ferdia?" I asked.

"I'll leave him with one of dockers here. He can take care of him until I come back."

He called over a big burly docker wearing a dirty grey overall.

"Murphy, mind this horse until I get back," he ordered.

Murphy grunted and took hold of Ferdia's reins.

"We have to go, now!" Seamus declared as the soldiers came closer.

We made our way over to the steps leading down to the boat. Ferdia tried to walk with us. Murphy was too strong for him and was able to hold him back.

"He doesn't want to leave you children!" Seamus laughed.

We went down the steps to the boat and climbed in. Seamus, some of his crew and Phelim started to row away from the pier just as the soldiers were closing in.

"We're anchored in Ringsend, so sit back and enjoy the view, young 'uns!" Seamus said.

I looked back and saw Ferdia standing erect and looking at us as we sailed away. Murphy was hanging on to him for dear life. By this time, they were surrounded by the soldiers who seemed to be asking Murphy some questions.

"Will they be all right?" I asked.

"Murphy has a special talent for getting in and out of trouble. He'll be fine!"

"What about Ferdia?"

The soldiers now were taking a special interest in the horse and it looked as if they were trying to take him away from Murphy, despite his protests.

"Looks like they want the horse," observed Seamus.

"Oh, no!" cried Aoife. "Captain Kelly left Ferdia in our care!"

Two of the soldiers grabbed the reins and started to pull Ferdia away from the side of the dock. Ferdia reared his legs but was forced backward as two more soldiers arrived to help.

"Stop!" Aoife shouted. *"We have to go back!"*

"We can't do anything, Aoife. Keep rowing, lads!" Seamus ordered.

As we rowed away we saw Ferdia break free from his captors who tried in vain to catch him. Then Murphy ran and leapt onto him and they both escaped.

We all cheered.

"I told you they could take care of themselves," Phelim said.

"That is one special horse!" Seamus said in admiration. "It's a pity the poor creature is stuck with you, Phelim!"

After a few minutes, Seamus grabbed me by the arm and pointed out to sea.

"There she is! Do you see her, out in the bay?"

I looked out and saw a large ship. "The one with three masts and white sails?" I asked.

Both Phelim and Seamus fell about laughing again.

"Th–three masts!" gasped Seamus.

"Wh–white sails!" roared Phelim.

"What's so funny?" I asked.

"That's one of Cromwell's finest ships!" Seamus grabbed my arm again. "Look again to the starboard, boy!"

I looked at Aoife in bewilderment.

"Look to the right of the ship, your left," she said.

A small ship with a single mast and torn yellow sails came into sight. It also had a hole at the bow.

"Is it the ship with a hole?" I asked. "Why does it have a hole?"

"Well, travelling by sea does have its fair share of dangers. That happened the last time we bumped into an English ship," Seamus said with a grin. "A misunderstanding – a cannon shot fired. Don't worry though, it's seaworthy."

"Are you sure?" I asked.

"Sure, we've survived so far!"

"Are you pirates?" I blurted out.

He looked at me for a moment and grinned again. "Some of the English like to call us that. We prefer the term 'privateers'. Our ship *The Lady Geraldine* is small, but it is fast. We haven't been caught yet!"

Privateer? I knew a privateer was a person who had permission from the government or king to capture enemy merchant ships and goods. A pirate with a license in other words! I doubted Seamus had one!

When we reached the ship we helped the crew to load on the supplies and got on board.

Phelim remained in the lighter.

"Are you sure you'll be all right rowing back on your own?" Seamus sneered.

"As long as you're not around, I'll be perfectly fine!" Phelim responded as he rowed away. "Good luck, children!" he shouted. "You'll need it with that nitwit!"

Seamus sighed. "He always has to have the last word." He turned to his crew. *"Lift anchor, lads! To Wexford!"*

As we headed out to sea, I looked out into the expanse ahead of us.

"Don't worry, lad," Seamus said. "We will be keeping quite close to the coast. The big English frigates can't get too close to us in here. We'll reach Wexford by tomorrow."

Chapter 4

Wexford, 1649

The sea was calm as we sailed through the night. As I looked up, I noticed the bright light again shining in the night sky. It seemed to be a little farther away now. I turned to Aoife to mention it to her, but she was fast asleep. I don't think the poor thing had slept at all in the last few days. Come to think of it, neither had I. My eyes grew heavy and I drifted off into a deep sleep.

As I slept I dreamt I could hear a woman's voice call to me.

"Liam, Liam, come back to us, Liam! Come back, my darling boy! Can you hear me? Please come back!" she pleaded.

I woke up with a start and looked around, thinking that perhaps the voice came from someone on the ship.

There was nobody there except the sailors and there certainly was no woman among them.

She had called me "my darling boy". Was it my mother? But if it was, why didn't I recognise her voice?

I tried to remember what had happened before I met Aoife in Drogheda, but it was very difficult to recall. There was something about a bus. Now what was a bus? For the life of me I couldn't remember! My memory was fading. I knew I'd got a bump on the head though I couldn't remember how that had happened.

Dawn was breaking.

Aoife opened her eyes and looked over at me. She smiled.

"Did you get a chance to sleep?" she asked.

"A little," I replied. "I dreamt I heard a woman's voice calling to me. I think she might have been my mother, but I can't be sure."

Aoife became very interested. "What did she say to you?"

"She begged me to come back to her."

"Did she tell you how to get back?"

"No – no, she didn't."

Aoife bit the lower part of her lip. I could tell she was deep in thought.

"Another thing – I saw that bright light in the sky again last night. But I think it's getting farther away."

Sudden shouts all over the ship brought us back to the present.

"Enemy on the portside!"

We heard the boom of a cannon.

"Brace for impact, lads!" came the roar.

A cannonball hit the ship with a sickening crash. There was an explosion and one of the young cabin boys was thrown overboard.

"Help, help! I can't swim!" he screamed as he struggled to keep his head above the water.

"Man overboard!" I yelled, but the rest of the crew were too busy trying to deal with the ship that was attacking us. *"We have to help him!"* I shouted to Aoife.

"But how? I can't swim!"

I spotted a rope on the deck. I grabbed one end of it and tied it to a rail on the side of the ship.

"What are you going to do?"

"I'm going to find out if five years of swimming lessons have been worthwhile!" Holding the other end of the rope, I dived into the water. The cold water hit me with full force, but I surfaced and began to tread water. I looked around to try and find the boy who had fallen in. I spotted him just a short distance away.

He went down below the surface twice, shouting and flailing his arms, desperately trying to swim. He was about to go down for the last time. I swam as hard as I could and reached him. I tried to hand him the rope, but he was panicking too much to realise what I was up to.

He grabbed me. He was going to drag both of us down! I took a deep breath as we sank under the water. As we sank deeper he stopped struggling, as if he had accepted his fate, and I managed to tie the rope around his waist. Then I swam up to the surface and pulled him up with me.

At this stage Aoife had a few sailors with her who realised what I was trying to do. They started to pull on the rope and, slowly but surely, they were able to pull the terrified cabin boy up onto the deck. A rope ladder was thrown down for me to climb on board.

By the time I climbed back on deck I was exhausted and very, very cold. Aoife wrapped me in a warm blanket. The cabin boy lay lifeless. He had swallowed a lot of water.

"Put him lying on his side," I shouted, *"and pump his arms!"*

They looked at me strangely but did what I asked. After a few minutes he coughed up some water and sat up, coughing and spluttering. He was shaken but alive.

Seamus rushed over to us. "That was a very brave thing you did there, lad!"

"Brave, but very very silly!" whispered Aoife.

"But for you, my only son Oisín would be lying at

the bottom of the sea," Seamus continued. "I am forever in your debt."

"Your s-s-s-son?" I asked through chattering teeth.

"Yes, lad, my son. His mother would never have forgiven me if anything happened to him." Tears began to fill his eyes and he turned away. "I would never have been able to forgive myself."

He hurried back to command his crew.

"That was a very dangerous thing to do," Aoife said sternly. "What were you thinking?"

"I don't know, I can't explain. I just knew that I would be all right."

"What made you think that?"

"You were here. For some reason I know as long as you are here nothing bad will happen to me."

Aoife hugged me, then gave me a thump on the arm.

"*Ow!* What's that for!"

"That's for scaring the life out of me!"

Then she hugged me again.

"What's *that* for?"

"That's for doing what you did. He would have drowned without your help."

A burst of cheering erupted from the crew.

"What's happening?" I asked one of the sailors.

"We've been able to outrun the English ship! We're out of their cannon range now, so we're safe for the moment!"

"For the moment? What does that mean? When will we get to Wexford?"

"We'll be there in a few hours."

We reached Rosslare early in the afternoon.

"Look up there, children – that's Rosslare fort," Seamus told us. "It guards the entrance to Wexford Harbour. As long as the Irish or Royalist supporters control it, none of Cromwell's ships will be able get into Wexford Harbour."

We docked at the harbour.

"Go to Wexford Castle," Seamus told us. "You may find the colonel there." He pointed to a castle with four towers that overlooked the harbour.

We said our goodbyes, with Seamus swearing again that he would be forever in my debt and that I could call on him for help at any time.

Aoife and I set out for the castle.

"The people have no idea what's coming," I said.

"You're right – let's hurry."

When we arrived at the castle gate it was guarded by a group of soldiers. One of them stepped forward and spoke to us in a very gruff manner.

"What's your business here?"

"We have a message from Commander Aston for

Colonel Sinnott."

"Oh yes, and I'm the Queen of Sheba!" he sneered.

Aoife and I looked at one another, confused.

"The Queen of where?" I asked.

"Are you being smart, boy?" he said threateningly.

A woman passing by with some children intervened.

"Stop being such an idiot, Ned Carmody! Let them in to see the colonel. They may be telling the truth."

"All right!" the soldier said sulkily.

"See you later then, brother!" the woman said as she walked away.

"Blooming sisters!" he muttered under his breath.

Aoife looked at me and smiled mischievously.

"What?" I asked.

"Just thinking – I've become something like your 'blooming sister', haven't I?'

"Yes, you *are* bossy, I must say!" I laughed. "But I like it!"

Carmody led us into the castle and up a stairway that led to a large room where a young man in uniform was sleeping in a chair.

"Sorry to disturb you, sir," the soldier began cautiously.

"Oh, what is it, Carmody? Can't you see I'm busy?" he yawned.

"These two children here claim to have a message from Commander Aston."

"Who?"

"Commander Aston from Drogheda, sir," I replied.

"Never heard of him, Carmody. Get these children out of my sight."

"Yes, Captain Stafford."

"But, captain, Cromwell and his army have taken Drogheda and are probably on their way here now," I pleaded.

The captain laughed. *"Stuff and nonsense!"* he roared.

"It's true, sir," Aoife said. "The commander and many others were killed in Drogheda. The commander asked us to find Colonel Sinnott."

"Why Colonel Sinnott?"

"He wanted us to warn him, sir. Commander Aston believed Cromwell would march along the coast supported by the navy and target Wexford," I continued.

Aoife looked at me, startled. "How did you know that?" she whispered.

"I don't know – it just came into my head," I whispered back.

"Even if what you say about Drogheda is true," said the captain, "he'll never reach us here without meeting a lot of opposition on the way. His army will be exhausted by the time they get here."

"Not so, captain," I said. "Cromwell has made it back to Dublin safely with his army without any opposition. People are afraid to challenge him after Drogheda!"

"We will get support from the Northern counties then!" barked the captain.

"I'm afraid not, sir," I continued. "Colonel Venables has captured Carlingford and Newry, and Antrim is now under the control of Sir Charles Coote. They are all loyal to Cromwell. There will be no assistance coming from the north. The only thing delaying him now is that he is visiting his wife in Dublin. He then plans to march on Wicklow and Wexford."

Aoife was looking at me, wide-eyed.

"I don't believe it!" said the captain, narrowing his eyes suspiciously. "How do you know all this?"

"I can't explain how I know. My memory is a little hazy. I think I did a school project about it."

"What's a school project?" Aoife asked.

"It's when your teacher gives you a topic to study at school and you have to do some research on it, and then write about what you found out."

Carmody and Captain Stafford looked at one another blankly, and then looked at me.

"Have you been sipping the wine, boy?" Captain Stafford asked. "You're not making sense! How could you 'find out' something that hadn't happened yet, you fool?"

"Look, you must believe me! For some reason, I do

know that he will be at the gates of your town by early October. I'm telling the truth!"

"But October's only three days away!" said Carmody.

"Well, he'll have to get past Enniscorthy Castle first!" Captain Stafford said.

"Enniscorthy will not stand in his way. They are no match for Cromwell's army and will surrender without a fight," I replied.

"Nonsense!" he said. "And we still control the sea!"

"Cromwell has a large navy sailing down the coast. They are carrying the large cannons and are providing assistance where he needs it. Your forces will be no match for them."

"Get these children out of here, Carmody. They try my patience!" the captain snapped. "The boy must have had a blow to the head."

He was right about that. Was my brain damaged?

"Yes, sir!" Carmody said. "Where will I put them?"

"Throw them out onto the street. It's the right place for ragamuffins like that, spreading false stories about Cromwell, hoping to frighten the people."

Carmody began to usher us out but was called back by the captain.

"Actually, on second thoughts, don't let these children anywhere near the streets spreading these wild stories. They might cause a panic!"

"What will I do with them, sir?"

"Lock them up. Put them in a cell and chain them up."

Carmody gaped at him. "But they're only children, sir. Are you sure?"

"Are you disobeying a direct order, Carmody?"

"No, sir!"

"You can't lock us up," I protested. "We're trying to help!"

Carmody drew his sword and forced us out of the room.

"Down those steps!" he ordered as we were led down to a cell.

"In you go!" he roared.

"You can't do this!" Aoife cried as she fell to her knees and grabbed Carmody by the legs. *"Please, let us out!"*

"Keep your mouth shut! Be thankful I don't chain you up the way the captain ordered. Now keep quiet and I'll try to get some food and water to you later. Look, I'm sorry about this, I really am, but orders are orders!"

He went out and locked the door of the cold, dark and damp cell.

The only light came from a grill in the wall which looked out onto Wexford Harbour.

"It's all right, Aoife, we'll be fine," I said.

"Oh, I know we will, Liam, I know we will!" She smiled as she held out a large key. "I've got the key to the cell!"

"*What?* How did you get it?"

"When I fell to my knees and grabbed Carmody I lifted it from his pocket! He never felt a thing!"

"Well, aren't you the clever one!" I laughed.

"Come on then!" She hurried to the door.

She put the key in the cell door and opened it without any problem.

"How will we get out though?" I asked.

"There must be a back door down here somewhere."

We ran down a dark corridor.

"Someone is coming!" I whispered as I heard the whistle of someone approaching. The door to a nearby cell was unlocked. "In here," I whispered, pushing Aoife inside.

We hid in the shadows at the back of the cell.

"*Who goes there?*" said a voice in the darkness.

"What are you on about?" said another voice.

"I thought I heard something."

"Nothing down here except some rats!"

"Rats!" whimpered Aoife.

"*Shhh!*" I whispered back.

"Did you hear that?" the first voice asked.

Aoife and I held our breath.

"It's nothing, I tell you – come on, let's get up to the captain! You know our lord and master doesn't like to be kept waiting!"

We heard their footsteps walking away and felt confident enough to breathe again.

"That was a close one!" Aoife sighed.

We both walked forward carefully in the darkness, and felt our way along the dank damp walls, looking for a way out.

Suddenly we saw a small chink of light.

"It's a door!" said Aoife.

We ran to it and I tried to pull it open. But it wouldn't budge.

"It's locked!" I said.

Then we heard someone on the other side fidgeting with the lock.

"There's someone coming in!" I said.

"We must hide!"

"No, we need to make sure the door stays open! We'll let him walk in and then we'll hit him on the head."

"Hit him with what?"

I felt around on the ground in the darkness and found a small rock.

"I have a rock," I whispered.

"A rock? Are you trying to kill him?"

"Of course not!"

"What if it's more than one person?" Aoife hissed.

Before I could answer the door was pushed open.

Somebody popped a head in.

"I told you I can pick any lock!" a voice said.

"Well, can you see anything?" another voice from outside asked.

"Would you give me a moment! I'm trying to adjust to the darkness."

I stood by the door, rock in hand.

"I blame you, pirate! I left those children in your care!"

"I'm not a nurse! I'm a businessman!"

I knew that grumpy voice – it was Phelim!

"Phelim!" I called.

"Phelim!" cried Aoife.

"Ghosts in the darkness! They know my name!" Phelim shouted.

"Saints preserve us, it's the children, you fool!" laughed Seamus.

Phelim stepped back outside and Aoife and I ran out into the street to freedom. Even though it was raining heavily, I was never so happy to see daylight!

"What are you doing here?" Aoife asked.

"We went to Captain Stafford looking for the two of you and he told us he had locked you up. We decided to try to get you out. Seamus here knows this prison like the back of his hand."

"I've been a resident here many times!" he laughed.

"That young captain is a right scoundrel!" Phelim declared.

"I've never trusted him," Seamus agreed. "There's something about him that doesn't ring true."

"How did you get to Wexford, Phelim?" I asked.

"Well, on Ferdia of course! Once we'd attracted all that attention at the Dublin docks we had to skedaddle. We knew you were going to Wexford, so we decided to follow!"

"Where is Ferdia?" Aoife asked.

"I have put him in some stables nearby. He didn't like it, but I didn't want to attract any attention. You know what that horse is like. He couldn't keep the head down or stay quiet if his life depended on it!"

"Speaking of keeping the head down, let's get away from here before they know we've escaped," I said. "We still need to find Colonel Sinnott. Besides, we're getting very wet in this rain!"

We moved off stealthily along the street.

"Imagine locking children up in a jail cell! That's a disgrace!" Seamus said angrily.

"Keep it down, man," Phelim said. "And let's get off these streets before we're seen."

"I know a tavern just a street or two away where we'll be safe," Seamus said.

"A tavern? But we're kids?" I said.

"Don't worry, lad – they serve children too!" he laughed.

I looked at him in horror. "I don't drink alcohol! I'm only nearly twelve!"

"I'm only joking. Lost your sense of humour in that cell, did you? They will let you smoke though, but only a small cigar," he chuckled.

"Tobacco is bad for you!" I said.

"What is it with the youth of today?" Seamus asked. "No alcohol, no tobacco? You'll be telling me to eat vegetables and drink more water next!"

"You could be the first vegetarian pirate!" I said.

"What's a vegetarian?" he asked.

"Stop jabbering!" said Aoife. "We need to *move*!"

We ran through the streets until we got to a tavern called Healy's. When the tavern owner saw us, he let us through to a room at the back where we would not be seen.

"I'm just going out front to check that the coast is clear," Seamus said after a minute or two.

"Oh yes, I think I'll go with you – just to check that the coast is clear also," Phelim said.

"And perhaps something for the thirst?" Seamus asked.

"Oh yes, a bird never flew on one wing," Phelim replied as he went with him.

"So, what now?" Aoife asked.

My stomach rumbled. "Well, we haven't eaten since yesterday!"

"I'm starving!"

Healy must have heard us as he soon brought us two goblets of milk and some bread and cheese.

"There you go, young'uns!" he smiled. "We have to

keep the troops fed and watered!"

"Oh yes, a bird never flew on one wing!" I replied.

"You're right there!" he said as he walked away laughing.

"A bird never flew on one wing?" Aoife asked.

I shrugged my shoulders. "Seemed to be the right thing to say!"

We gulped down the food and drink.

"Right. We have to get to the colonel before it's too late!" I declared.

"How do we find him?" Aoife asked.

"Well, that's easy," Seamus said as he came back in, holding his drink. "The colonel normally visits the captain to make sure everything is in good order. The captain hates it! All we have to do is stay close to the castle and we'll find the colonel!"

Healy entered with a worried look on his face.

"I've just been outside. The soldiers from the castle are searching each building."

"Looks like they've realised you've escaped," Seamus said as he scratched his ear. "We need a more secure hiding place."

"I've got a basement the soldiers don't know about," Healy suggested.

"Lead on!" Phelim commanded.

Carrying a tall candle in a candlestick, Healy led us down a dark and narrow stairwell into a room full of barrels. Some were marked porter, others whiskey, others wine.

In the candlelight I could see the eyes of Seamus and Phelim light up at the contents of the room.

"Now, lads," Healy pleaded, "I'm trusting you not to open the barrels."

"Well, the very notion of it!" Phelim replied. "To even think that we would stoop to that sort of behaviour! What kind of people do you think we are?"

Healy grunted and, putting the candlestick down on a barrel, left us in the basement.

"Well now, which barrel do you want to sample first?" Seamus asked Phelim.

"You promised that you wouldn't open them!" Aoife said.

"Oh, we won't open them, I guarantee that," Phelim said. "Our word is our bond! Isn't that right, Seamus?"

"Oh, that's right – we're just going to make a little hole in the side and have a little taste and then seal it up again with some cloth. No opening involved at all!"

Before the men got the chance to tackle a barrel, a shout came from above.

"They're here! Cromwell's soldiers are here!"

We raced out of the basement and up to the pub. It didn't matter who saw us now.

A young boy was talking excitedly to Healy.

"That's right, I saw them! They're just a mile or so

away now. They say Enniscorthy Castle surrendered without a fight. Cromwell's got his sights on Wexford next, and he's got the navy as well to help him!"

There was a loud commotion outside. We looked out and saw groups of soldiers filling the square.

"The colonel's men – getting ready for the fray, I suppose," Healy said.

"He's a clever man, that colonel," Seamus observed. "He'll try to avoid a fight for as long as he can. He knows it's still raining heavily out there. Cromwell's army must be wet to the bone and very tired at this stage. The longer he holds out, the better the chance that Cromwell and his army will go somewhere drier and more comfortable!"

"Aye, he'll want Wexford as a base where his army can rest and see out the winter, while he prepares his plan of attack for the rest of the country," Phelim said.

"That's not the only reason he's coming here," Healy observed. "He thinks some of the local inhabitants are pirates and are attacking English ships and stealing their goods."

We all looked at Seamus.

"Pirates? I've told you before we prefer the term *'privateers'*! We're not pirates, just businessmen! We only rob supporters of Cromwell. Some of the Irish and English actually support what we do, because it annoys Cromwell so much!"

"Well, whatever you call yourself, you can be sure Cromwell and his army will be searching for people like you!" Aoife replied.

"You children have a very worrying habit of speaking the truth!" laughed Seamus. "I'm not worried. If it keeps raining as heavily as this, it will slow down Cromwell's march and help spread the 'country sickness' amongst the soldiers."

Phelim nodded his head in agreement.

"What's that?" I asked.

"Dysentery," he replied. "Serious stomach upsets. Very unpleasant!"

"*Colonel Sinnott is approaching!*" a voice shouted from outside.

We raced outside to see him.

"*Colonel! Colonel!*" Aoife and I shouted as we ran towards him.

We were blocked from reaching him by Captain Stafford and his guards who were standing nearby.

"*Colonel!*" I shouted as soldiers grabbed me.

"*Be quiet, boy!*" Captain Stafford roared as I struggled to escape.

Seamus intervened.

"Let go of those children now, Stafford," he growled at the captain, "if you value your life and your position."

"How dare you speak to me in that manner! I will

have you locked up for your insolence!" Captain Stafford sneered.

"It will take a lot more than you and your pathetic group here to lock me up, Stafford." And he pointed to where the crew of his ship were approaching.

It looked like there was going to be a skirmish between the sailors and the soldiers.

"We shouldn't be fighting amongst ourselves!" I shouted. *"Cromwell is the one we should be united against!"*

"Well spoken, young man!" said Colonel Sinnott who had by now become aware of the conversation. "We should be all fighting as one. Now what is going on here?"

"These two brats escaped from my cell today!" Captain Stafford blustered.

"Did they indeed? And why would you have two children in a cell?" Colonel Sinnott asked.

"Why, sir?" Captain Stafford replied nervously.

"Yes, why would you lock up two children?" asked Phelim in a very mischievous tone.

"Well, they were causing trouble, sir!" replied the captain.

"Causing trouble, eh?" the colonel repeated. "Bring the two children here to me. Now then, what do you two have to say for yourselves. Have you been *fermenting disquiet* in the town?"

"Begging your pardon, sir," Aoife replied, "but I don't even know what that means."

The colonel laughed heartily and looked at me. "And what about you?"

"We were only trying to see you, sir – that's why the captain locked us up!" I pleaded. "We were sent by Commander Aston from Drogheda!"

The colonel's face darkened. "Commander Aston, you say? Why did he send you to me?"

"Well, sir, before he died …" I paused.

"Go on now, go on," the colonel urged.

I handed him the letter from Commander Aston. "Before he died, he asked us to find you and give you this letter to warn you about the danger of Cromwell and his army. The commander thought that Wexford would be the next big town Cromwell would attack."

"One of Aston's men reached me just before you did. Your message confirms what he told me," the colonel replied. "His army is right on our doorstep, and there are more of his forces due to arrive tomorrow. Not to mention the navy that he has waiting outside in the harbour for us."

"Surely they'll never get past the defence at Rosslare Harbour, Colonel?" Phelim said.

The colonel sighed. "Too late. The soldiers defending the fort have fled already. Cromwell will have a safe passage to sail right into Wexford."

"What's wrong in having them here?" a voice in the crowd asked. "We never wanted you Royalists here anyway!"

"That's right! Sure you're only newcomers yourselves!" another voice agreed.

"Not everyone in this town supports the colonel. Some would prefer to see Cromwell take over the town peacefully," Healy said.

"The people are afraid of what Cromwell might do if they don't surrender," Phelim mused.

"They are right to be afraid," I replied. "Aoife and I have seen the death and the destruction they can bring to a town."

"This is just the kind of talk that unsettles people!" Captain Stafford said. "That is why I locked them up. For public safety!"

"Well, public safety or not, we do not lock children up!" said the colonel. "By my order they are to be set free."

"Yes, sir," the captain reluctantly agreed.

"On the other hand, I don't want two children running around the town in dangerous times such as these," the colonel continued.

"Don't worry, Colonel, we will take care of them," Phelim said.

"We will, Colonel." Seamus nodded his head.

The town square was by now packed with even

more people, led by the mayor and other prominent people.

"Colonel, we do not want to end up fighting Cromwell and his army. We are no match for them," the mayor declared.

"Don't worry, Mr Mayor, the last thing I want to do is fight them," the colonel agreed. "At least not until I get more reinforcements. The wall surrounding the town is safe. There's no way they can get in without taking the castle first, and I have full confidence in Captain Stafford and his crew."

Everyone stared at Stafford who looked around nervously at the crowd.

"You can rely on me and my men, sir," he then said. "We won't let you down!"

"Good man!" the colonel replied as he turned to leave. "We must assume the rest of Cromwell's army will be here tomorrow. They won't attack until then, or at least not until they have their cannons in position."

"Cannons?" the captain asked timidly.

"Well, yes, of course, captain. What did you think they had? Pitchforks?"

All the people laughed.

"You and your men get back to the castle now, Stafford. I've got work to do."

"Are you thinking about your plan of attack, sir?" I asked.

"No, I'm thinking about terms of surrender actually," he replied with a wink as he walked away.

"What an interesting chap!" said Phelim.

"Interesting or not, he's going to get us all killed," the mayor replied.

He turned to the crowd.

"People of Wexford!" he declared. *"We need to show Cromwell that we mean him no harm and do not wish to fight!"*

Many in the crowd nodded their heads in approval.

Just then I noticed Captain Stafford slipping quietly away.

"Where is he off to?" Aoife asked.

"Back to the castle, no doubt," I replied. "I still don't trust him!"

"Your instincts are true," Seamus said. "Take my advice, young fella, never turn your back on that one. No matter what happens, he'll save himself and his cronies for sure."

"So, what do we do now?" I asked.

"Not much we can do tonight," Phelim said. "I suggest a good night's sleep. Who knows what tomorrow will bring?"

"You can stay in my place," Healy said.

We all agreed. I felt very tired. I knew Aoife was exhausted too, as she had fallen quiet.

As we left, the mayor was busy talking to some of

the crowd that remained. They were planning what they would do to get into Cromwell's good books.

"I don't blame them," Seamus said. "They don't want to get caught in a struggle between Cromwell and Colonel Sinnott."

When we reached the tavern Aoife and I were shown to a bedroom with two small beds. I lay down and fell asleep as soon as I hit the pillow.

During the night I had the dream again. I could hear a woman's voice calling me again, more distant this time, begging me to come to her. It might have been my mother. I wasn't sure. My memory of her was fading even more. I could not understand why. I dreamt the bright light in the sky was moving even farther away from me. It was now just a distant glow. What was happening?

As expected, the next morning we heard news that the rest of Cromwell's army had arrived.

"It's still raining," Seamus remarked as he looked out the window. "Cromwell and his army won't like that!"

The day passed without incident.

On the 3rd October, messengers from Cromwell arrived and declared that the people and soldiers in

Wexford would not be harmed if the town agreed to surrender without a fight.

Many people in the town were still in favour of this, but Colonel Sinnott decided to play for time.

"There are more reinforcements on the way," he told us when he visited later that day. "I don't want to show my hand too quickly, before I get the extra soldiers I need."

In the meantime, some of the townsfolk started sending supplies to the army outside. They sent food, water and beer.

As the days passed, there was an air of disquiet about the town.

"The calm before the storm," Phelim observed. "He won't wait forever, you know."

The colonel's expected reinforcements arrived – another 500 soldiers. This prompted the colonel to try and wait even longer.

"I know most of the people in the town do not support the fight against Cromwell," he admitted, "so I will try and keep the negotiations going for as long as I can."

We saw no sign of Captain Stafford or his soldiers in the coming days.

"They're hiding under their beds!" Seamus joked.

"It's no joking matter," Phelim warned. "If Stafford buckles, the whole town is doomed."

"Surely he wouldn't dare?" I said.

"When a person's life is on the line, you can never be sure how they are going to react in an effort to save their own skin," Phelim remarked drily.

Letters of negotiation went back and forth between Cromwell and Sinnot over the coming days. Still there was no battle.

"These days of peaceful negotiations have to end sometime. Cromwell's patience won't last forever!" Seamus remarked.

He was right.

On the 10th October Cromwell moved his cannons to the southern part of the town and fired a shot into Wexford Castle. That got everyone's attention.

Colonel Sinnott immediately sent word that he was willing to consider surrender terms with Cromwell. Negotiations for a surrender began.

While this was happening some of Cromwell's soldiers suddenly appeared at the top of the castle. Colonel Sinnott's soldiers who had been patrolling the town walls immediately fled as soon as they saw this.

"The castle has fallen! The scoundrel Stafford has sold his soul to the devil Cromwell and doomed us all!" Seamus roared. *"Look! They are coming, they are coming! Run, children!"*

The soldiers were climbing down the wall with ladders and killing anyone who stood in their way.

They were in a frenzy. Anyone caught in the square was killed immediately.

"Get to my ship, children!" Seamus cried, drawing his sword as he raced back to tackle the soldiers.

"Seamus, no!" I shouted, but to no avail.

He was soon swallowed up by hordes of Cromwell's soldiers.

"Come on, children!" Phelim urged. "There's no time to lose."

As Cromwell's men made their way through the town the soldiers who were defending the place ran away in fear and were chased down and killed. Any priests or friars who stood in their way were killed immediately.

"They have the blood lust upon them!" Phelim shouted. *"They're killing anyone who stands in their way. There's no stopping them!"*

We soon discovered that our way to the dockside was blocked by Cromwell's soldiers, so we followed the crowd as they ran towards the River Slaney.

"We may be able to get across the river to safety!" Phelim panted as we ran.

When we arrived at the river there were some small boats there, but they were overloaded with people. More and more were trying to get on board too, desperate to escape.

"There's too many people on the boats!" Aoife cried.

71

"They'll never make it!"

"You're right, child! Step back, step back!" Phelim shouted.

As we stepped away from the riverbank there was a scream from Aoife. She was being dragged towards one of the small boats by the panicking crowd.

"Aoife!" I yelled.

Aoife was pushing against the crowd but there were just too many of them.

"To the boats!" they kept shouting, *"To the boats!"*

"Aoife is trapped in the crowd, Phelim!" I shouted.

We tried to fight our way through the crowd, but we kept getting pushed back.

"There's too many of them, lad!" Phelim shouted. "We'll have to try another way. I hope this works!"

He put two fingers in his mouth and let out a loud whistle.

"What are you up to?" I asked desperately. "We must get Aoife!"

Phelim just stood there, hands on hips.

"Phelim!"

He whistled again.

Suddenly loud neighs pierced the air. Within seconds a horse appeared. The people all made way, fearful that it belonged to one of Cromwell's men.

It was Ferdia!

"Never fails!" said Phelim. "He was stabled nearby.

Come on, lad! Ferdia is making a path for us through the people. We can grab Aoife!"

Phelim and I were able to reach Aoife. She had been crushed by the crowd and was very dazed.

I was very worried. "Aoife, are you all right?"

"I'll be fine," she whispered. "Just need to catch my breath."

"Grab that horse!" a voice shouted.

"Come on, Aoife, let's get you onto Ferdia," Phelim said as some of the crowd started to draw closer. "He'll take you to safety."

Phelim helped her up onto the saddle and put the reins in her hands.

"Hold on now!" he shouted as he patted Ferdia on the flank. He galloped away before the crowd could reach him.

"Where will he take her?" I asked.

"A safe place," Phelim replied. "Don't worry – he'll make sure Aoife escapes without harm. Now, as for us, that's a different matter! I don't like the look of some of the people in this crowd!"

A number of men were approaching us, hate and fear in their eyes.

How are we going to get out of this? I wondered.

"Come on, you lazy lumps! Why are you hanging around here looking for trouble?" called a voice from behind.

"Seamus!" I shouted as I ran to him and gave him a huge hug.

"Ouch, careful there, young fella! I've got a scratch or two thanks to those New Model Army brutes!"

I looked at him. He had a large cut on his left cheek, his left arm was bloodied, and part of his right ear had been cut off.

"What happened your ear?" I asked.

"It had a close encounter with an English sword!"

"He hardly listens anyway so he won't miss one ear!" Phelim joked.

"That's funny coming from you, Mr Mighty Mouth!" Seamus replied.

"Can we do this another time? We really should get out of here!" I said.

"You're right, Liam," Seamus replied. "We need to move now! The soldiers are only minutes away. We need to get to my ship."

"But the harbour is under Cromwell's control!" I said.

"Don't worry, lad, the ship is down the coast at Waterford, waiting for us."

"How are Colonel Sinnott's troops faring against Cromwell's men?" Phelim asked.

"Colonel Sinnott is dead and Cromwell's soldiers are destroying the town," Seamus replied. "If we don't get moving we'll be dead too. But I'll tell you one thing, Phelim, after the treachery shown today the name of Captain Stafford will never be forgotten."

"What has happened to him?" I asked

"I don't know. If we meet him again, there will be no mercy shown. Justice will be swift," Phelim promised.

We moved away from the river and trekked across country.

"We'll head to New Ross first – I have some friends there who owe me a few favours. They will give us food and shelter," Seamus said. "It's a twenty-mile trek so we'd better move. It's probably next on Cromwell's list once he's finished here with Wexford."

"What about Ferdia and Aoife?" I asked.

As if on cue, they appeared over the top of a hill.

They came galloping down and, when they reached us, Aoife jumped off the horse and raced to me.

"Are you all right?" I asked as she tried to squeeze the life out of me with a huge hug.

"I'm fine," she said. "Ferdia got me out of any trouble." She looked at the three of us. "Poor Seamus! You've been through a war of your own."

"You should see the fellas on the other side!" he joked.

"Well, let me clean you up a little bit," Aoife replied.

"That can wait until New Ross, lass, I'll be fine. There's no time to waste. We don't know when those blasted soldiers are going to appear."

We started to walk towards New Ross. We insisted Seamus sit on the horse because of his injuries. Eventually he agreed.

"I'd be safer on my own two feet," he mumbled. "That horse has a mind of its own!"

"I'm glad you're all right," I whispered to Aoife.

"And, sure, why wouldn't I be?" she replied. "Nothing is going to happen to me, Liam. My job is to get you back safely, and that I will do."

"Back? Back where?" Again, I realised that everything before meeting her was a blur to me.

"Now where would be the fun in that if I told you? You'll have to wait and see!" she teased.

As we walked on we looked back at the boats on the river and the people on the riverside. The boats on the river, which were packed with people, were starting to sink. Many of the people could not swim and they were screaming for help.

"Don't look back," Aoife said to me. "You cannot help them, and you cannot change what has happened."

"But they'll drown," I said, as tears came to my eyes.

"I'm sorry, but you must listen to me. We have to get to New Ross and then see where that leads us. Trust me, Liam, this is what is best for you."

I stopped to look into her eyes. I could see that she

was telling the truth, but I still did not understand what she was talking about. That understanding did not come until much later.

We arrived without further incident at New Ross where we stayed with Seamus's friends. After a few nights' sleep and a few days' good food, Aoife and I recovered our health and spirits. Seamus too was in better health after some very firm nursing from the grandmother of the house. She refused to let him leave the bed despite his protests!

"Well, I never thought I would live to see the day!" Phelim laughed. "Finally someone who can control Seamus!"

"She does not control me!" Seamus retorted as he tried to get out of the bed to prove his point.

The grandmother appeared immediately. "Get yourself back under those covers at once! You're no good to man nor beast until you rest and recover!"

Seamus meekly obeyed.

Aoife and I looked at one another and sniggered.

"What news from Wexford?" he asked, trying to change the subject.

"Not good," Phelim replied. "Worse than Drogheda, they are saying. Thousands killed. Many others have fled. The town is under the control of Cromwell's army. They were so out of control they destroyed a lot of the town, so the army can't stay there."

"He was probably looking to stay in Wexford with the army for the winter," Seamus replied. "He won't be able to do that now."

"Apparently he was close to agreeing a peaceful surrender with Colonel Sinnott when Captain Stafford let the soldiers in and they ran riot," Phelim continued.

"Curse him!" Seamus said.

"Is Cromwell on his way here to New Ross?" Aoife asked.

"Yes, he's nearly here. I've spoken to the New Ross governor, Sir Lucas Taaffe, and told him what happened in Wexford. He's not going to take any chances."

"You mean he's going to surrender?" I said.

"Without a doubt," Phelim replied.

"Can't blame him, I suppose," said Seamus. "He doesn't want another Drogheda or Wexford. We'll want to be moving on to Waterford to get to my ship."

"You'll not be going anywhere," the grandmother screeched, *"until the doctor says you are fit to go!"*

"How does she keep appearing every time I talk about getting out of bed?" Seamus demanded.

"She must have magic powers!" Phelim joked.

A few more days passed.

Then we heard the sound of cannon outside.

"Are they shelling the town?" Aoife asked.

"Well, I would be surprised if they were," Phelim replied. "Probably just a warning to the governor to hurry up with the surrender."

A town crier appeared in the street below.

"People of New Ross, hear me now! The honourable Governor Taaffe of New Ross and General Cromwell have agreed peaceful terms of surrender. To avoid an effusion of blood, the town will agree not to engage with Cromwell in any act of war. All soldiers are to pack their bags immediately and leave the town in an orderly fashion. They will be allowed to take their weapons with them. Cromwell guarantees that the people of the town will not suffer injury or violence at the hands of his soldiers!"

"Right!" said Seamus, throwing back the covers and swinging his legs to the floor. "That's my cue for getting out of here."

"Why not stay for a few more days?" I suggested.

"Once Cromwell and his soldiers are here they might take a closer look at people like me, and my, shall we say, business activities. Oh no, now is the time to go – but you children should stay – it should be safer here."

"Oh no," Aoife chimed in. "We're seeing this through to the end. We have to warn all of the other towns about Cromwell."

"What good will that do?" Seamus asked.

"Well, at least they'll have the information to hand that will help them to decide whether to fight or surrender," I said.

"Sounds like you have it all figured out!" Phelim remarked.

Just as Seamus finished dressing himself, the grandmother reappeared.

"Where do you think you are going?" she roared at him.

Seamus grabbed her hand and gave her a kiss on the cheek.

"Thank you, dear lady, for your kind assistance. Now my friends and I must move on before Cromwell and his soldiers arrive. You have been my angel watching over me. I would not have recovered without you."

The lady blushed and smiled. "If I were forty years younger, I wouldn't be letting you out of my sight ever!"

Now it was Seamus's turn to blush.

"We really need to go," he muttered.

We hurried to grab the few belongings we had accumulated by now – like the warm hooded cloak the family had given Aoife and the cloak and broad-brimmed black hat I had been given. Meanwhile the grandmother quickly packed some food and drinks for us.

When we went outside, the street was already thronged with many soldiers who were taking the opportunity to leave peacefully.

"Let's move into the middle of the crowd," Seamus suggested. "We don't want to stand out too much, just in case anyone takes a special interest in us."

"What about Ferdia?" Aoife asked.

"One moment," Phelim said, and he whistled.

Ferdia appeared within moments and walked beside us.

"Where does he go?" I asked.

"No idea!" Phelim replied. "But he always turns up when I whistle!"

Seamus shook his head in amazement. "Have you ever heard of a horse that comes when you whistle, young 'uns? That horse thinks he's a dog!"

When we reached the edge of the town we met Cromwell's troops.

"Just keep walking," Seamus whispered. "They won't be interested in us."

Many of the soldiers looked ill.

"We can thank the Irish weather for that," Phelim said when I mentioned it to him. "The cold and wet weather are providing more of an obstacle to them than the people of Ireland."

As we were just about to leave the army behind us, I spotted a sickly figure sitting on a horse, calmly looking at the sight before him. It was Cromwell himself! He had a blanket over his shoulders and looked very pale and was shivering.

"Look over there," I whispered, not wishing to draw attention.

"I see him," Aoife replied. "Let's keep walking."

"It's malaria, I've seen it before," Seamus said. "He won't be going anywhere for a few weeks until he sees it out. That's if he ever sees it out."

"True," Phelim said. "Even if he gets through this, once you get malaria, there is always the chance it will come back at different times during your life."

"Malaria? In Ireland?" I said, confused. "I thought you could only get that in tropical countries?"

"Well, you thought wrong," said Phelim.

I looked directly at Cromwell as we passed by. I couldn't take my eyes off him. I felt that I was transfixed. He looked at me directly and was trying to speak.

"I have granted the people of New Ross a seasonable mercy. I do not take the lives of others lightly," he muttered. Then he fell forward on his horse and some of his aides rushed to assist him.

"Come on, lad," Phelim urged. "We need to keep moving."

Ferdia nudged me with his nose as if to say, 'Keep walking'. I got the message.

Chapter 5

Waterford, 1649

We reached Waterford in a few days and Seamus left us to meet up with his crew and ship.

That evening we sat down for something to eat in a tavern. I felt very tired.

"Aren't you hungry, lad?" Phelim asked me after noticing that I hadn't touched my meal.

"Will you leave me alone!" I snapped. "I'll eat when and where I want. I don't need you lecturing me all of the time!"

"Liam, is everything all right?" Aoife asked.

"I'm fine," I said. "I'm not hungry, but I feel cold. Can we get a fire on in here?"

Aoife touched my forehead. "You're freezing!" she said in alarm.

"I-I th-think I've picked up a cold," I stammered.

"And my head hurts. I think if I can lie down for a few minutes, I'll be fine."

I tried to get up but fell to the ground.

I don't remember too much about the following days. I was lying in bed, feeling the chills one minute, then feeling very hot and sweating, then the chills again. Every part of my body ached.

I went in and out of consciousness during that time. I was aware of Aoife watching over me, speaking softly to me, wiping my face with a cloth and holding my hand. From time to time I could see Phelim or Seamus. I even saw Ferdia at one stage, but I'm sure that was a dream. I could hear a woman's voice calling my name over and over again.

Then, I woke one morning and sat up in the bed.

Aoife was sitting on a chair beside me.

"How are you feeling?" she said.

"I feel much better, thanks," I said. "What happened?"

"The doctor thinks it was malaria. Can I get you anything?"

"I'm starving. I didn't have the dinner last night."

"Last night? That was two weeks ago!"

"Two weeks?" I shouted, getting out of the bed. My legs buckled under me.

"No getting out of bed yet, you still need to rest. You're still very weak."

"How long do I have to stay in the bed?" I asked.

"A few weeks, young lad, or as long as the doctor prescribes," said Phelim as he entered the room.

"But –" I started.

"No buts! You won't be getting out until you've recovered fully!" Phelim insisted.

"Now I know how Seamus felt!" I said. "Speaking of Seamus, where is he?"

"He's fine. He met up with his ship and crew. They're getting ready to sail. We have heard that Cromwell will be on his way to Waterford soon, so they don't want to stay around any longer than necessary."

"I'll go and get you some soup," Aoife said, rising from her chair.

"Phelim, I want to say sorry to you for the way I spoke to you the other night, I mean two weeks ago, at the dinner table. I was very rude."

"Don't worry about that, lad, it's the malaria. It makes a person irritable. Cromwell himself still has a bad bout of it, and he is in a foul humour because of it!" He chuckled. "His illness has slowed him down. A lot of the army are sick as well, so that gives us some breathing space."

"What about the rest of the country?" I asked. "Are the other towns going to oppose him?"

"The news is not good. The one leader who might

have rallied the troops, Owen Roe O'Neill, has died. The Governor of Cork, Sir Robert Starling, has been overthrown by a group who support Cromwell, so they won't block Cromwell's progress. Other towns will soon follow Cork's example and be in the hands of Cromwell supporters very soon."

"Don't be filling his head with bad news, he needs to rest," Aoife declared as she returned to the room with a bowl of hot soup and some bread.

"I feel much better, honest!" I said.

However, as soon as I had finished my soup I felt very hot and feverish, and fell into another cycle of sleeping and waking and dreaming without any definite sense of where I was or what was happening.

A few days later I woke again, feeling much better.

Seamus was in the room this time.

"Where's Aoife?" I asked.

"I sent her to bed. She's been caring for you these past few weeks, without any rest herself. The poor girl is completely worn out." He gave me some water and a few small pieces of bread to eat. "Take your time now," he advised. "Your body needs to adjust to food and drink again."

I fell asleep again after my small meal, but this time I slept peacefully and without any disturbing dreams.

I was up and about after a few days and slowly regained my strength. The weather was not very good, so I was forced to stay indoors.

"There's no point in you going outside in that harsh November weather and getting ill again," Aoife pointed out.

"Luckily, this bad weather will slow Cromwell down further," I observed.

"I'm sure you're right," Phelim said as he entered the room. "How are you feeling today, lad?"

"A lot better, thanks."

"That's good, because we may need to leave at short notice. Cromwell's army has captured Passage Fort on the west side of the harbour. That means his ships can now bring in the heavy guns to attack Waterford."

"He hasn't had it all his own way though," Seamus added. "The forces at Duncannon, on the east side of the harbour, have been able to hold out against the army commanded by Henry Ireton, Cromwell's son-in-law."

"Even if they try and bring in the heavy guns, won't the ground be too wet and soggy to support their weight?" I asked.

"That may well be the case, especially if this rain keeps up," he replied. "Liam, lad, you continue to surprise me. Your grasp of the situation often seems beyond your years."

"True," said Phelim. "And for that very reason I

have brought a guest to see you – you and Aoife – if you are feeling up to it?"

"A guest?" I asked, looking at Aoife. "Fine with me."

Phelim went outside and brought in an important-looking man dressed in a military uniform.

"Good morning, children," he said. "I hope you will pardon the intrusion. I am Colonel Lyvett, the Governor of Waterford. I was hoping that I could talk to you both for a few minutes?"

Aoife and I nodded our heads in agreement. What does the Governor of Waterford want with us? I wondered.

As if he read my mind, he said, "You have been through a lot, and I was hoping you could tell me about all you have been through over the last few months. You may have heard that Cromwell is outside the town. We have agreed a five-day truce while we negotiate a possible surrender. It would help if you could share your experiences with me. The more I know about this man and his methods the better."

We spent the next few hours telling the governor everything we knew. When the conversation was over, he thanked us and rose to leave.

"Governor, what do you think you will do?" I asked him.

He looked at me earnestly. "I do not know for sure, Liam. We do not want our people to be killed, and yet we know that Cromwell's army is suffering at the moment. Many soldiers are sick with malaria or dysentery. He may not have the might to take the city without a large number of casualties. We also have an added advantage he is not aware of."

"What advantage?" I asked.

"For your own safety I cannot tell you that. Suffice it to say, there may be help on the way. So, for the moment, we will keep up the negotiations with Cromwell until we have no other option."

"Thank you, Governor," Aoife said.

"It should be me thanking you, children. Your information will be invaluable in the days to come. Now I know exactly what we are facing."

We found out a few days later what he meant by help being on the way, when an extra 1,500 soldiers, led by Lieutenant-General Richard Farrell entered the town.

The month of December rolled in. I had not been out of the house in weeks. By the 2nd December I decided that I just had to get out into the air.

"All right," Aoife agreed. "Make sure to wrap up

warm. Here are some fresh clothes, courtesy of the lady of the house."

I got dressed. Then we put on our cloaks, I jammed my hat down on my head and we set off for the harbour.

"Where are the ships?" I asked.

Aoife looked at me blankly. "The ships?"

As I looked around I realised I could not see any soldiers either.

"They're gone! They're gone!" I shouted.

We raced back into the town, shouting *"They're gone!"*

When we got to the house, Phelim and Seamus came running out to meet us.

"What's that?" Seamus asked. "Who's gone?"

"Cromwell!" I shouted.

"Are you still feverish?" Seamus asked. "How could he be gone?"

"No, it's true!" Aoife said. "They must have gone during the night!"

"Well, that's the best piece of news I've heard in months!" Seamus chuckled.

"Is he retreating?" Aoife asked hopefully.

"Unlikely," I replied. "A combination of the bad weather, illness among his soldiers and the extra soldiers in the town have forced him to change his mind about taking Waterford. He knows there won't be a surrender and he wants to avoid a battle until his soldiers have recovered. He'll head towards Cork. He knows he has support there."

"There you go again," Phelim said in wonder. "How do you know all this?"

"School project," Aoife replied, smirking.

"Of course," Phelim replied.

"Do you know what a school project is?" Aoife asked him.

Phelim began to stutter. "Well, of course I do – it's a – it's a –"

"Ha! Not often we see you stuck for a word or two!" Seamus laughed.

"Well, if you're so clever, perhaps you might explain it to Phelim?" Aoife suggested.

Now it was the turn of Seamus to become flustered, but he quickly recovered.

"No point in showing off, I don't want to embarrass the man with my superior knowledge! You're probably right, Liam," he changed the conversation. "Cromwell will probably let the army rest for a while in Cork before undertaking any more conquests just yet."

Cromwell's army rested for the months of December and January. We rested too. There was nothing we could do anyway with the bad weather and the sickness that prevailed. We did not see Seamus during that time. He was away with his crew.

During this time I still had dreams of a woman calling to me, but they were becoming less frequent.

By February word reached us that Cromwell and his army were marching through Tipperary without too much resistance and had taken Fethard and Cashel. Again, it looked as if nobody could stop him.

One night there was a loud bang on the door.

Seamus rushed in with a letter. *"Traitor, that dirty traitor! How could he do this to his own people! His own people!"* he shouted.

"What is it, Seamus?" I asked.

"It's Kilkenny! It has been betrayed by an officer!"

"Not again!" I said. "You mean like Captain Stafford in Wexford?"

"Not exactly, lad – Cromwell hasn't arrived there yet!"

"What do you mean?" said Aoife. "How can that be?"

"You need to tell us exactly what has happened," I said.

"Yes, you're right of course. I'm getting a bit carried away. Perhaps a small glass of porter would help to settle my nerves."

Aoife fetched him a glass which Seamus drank in one gulp.

"Now, where was I?" he asked.

"*Betrayed!*" I said.

"Oh yes, betrayed, by a scoundrel officer Captain Tickle who is part of the town garrison."

"How do you know he has betrayed the town?" I asked.

"One of my lads intercepted a letter from him to Cromwell where he offers to help Cromwell to get into Kilkenny through one of the gates," Seamus replied.

"Intercepted? What do you mean intercepted?" I asked. "How did you get your hands on his letter?"

"Well!" he shrugged, reluctant to say more.

"Are you opening people's letters?" Aoife asked.

"I wouldn't quite say that. It's more like checking letters for items that may be of interest in the battle against Cromwell."

"But how do you know if a letter is of interest?" I asked.

"Well, by opening it and finding out of course!"

"Perhaps it's best if you don't tell us any more about how you got this," Aoife suggested.

"I think that might be best," Seamus replied. "Some secrets are best kept ... secret!"

"What's so important about Kilkenny?" Aoife asked.

"It's the family home of the Earl of Ormonde, the leader of the Royalist forces in Ireland," I replied. "He is regarded as the king's representative and he has a castle there. It would be a big boost to Cromwell if he succeeded in taking it, and a big blow to the Royalist forces."

"You're a fountain of knowledge, Liam!" Seamus chuckled.

"So, what are we going to do?" I asked.

"Well, what can we do?" Phelim replied. "Cromwell is going to take Kilkenny with or without Tickle's help."

"Yes," Aoife agreed. "But that doesn't mean we have to make it easy for him, does it? Come on, Liam, we have to head for Kilkenny."

I got up and stood at the door with Aoife. We both looked at Seamus and Phelim, who looked at one another.

"Well, I suppose we could make the effort," Phelim suggested, looking at Seamus.

"That's the spirit!" Seamus replied. "I was hoping you would say that! I took the liberty of having some horses ready for us, just in case!"

We packed some saddlebags, wrapped ourselves in our cloaks and went outside.

There, Ferdia was waiting with three other horses.

"You mount Ferdia," Aoife said to me. "You're the one we need to keep safe."

"Why do you keep saying that? I want you to be safe too."

"Don't worry about me, Liam! There will come a day when I will need you but, until then, jump up on Ferdia, and let's be off!"

Chapter 6

Kilkenny, 1650

We arrived at Kilkenny after two days without incident. The town was bracing itself for Cromwell's arrival. His army had defeated the forces at Gowran Castle which was just fifteen miles away and was fast approaching.

"What do you want?" we were asked by one of the guards at the gate to the town.

"We need to see the person in charge," Seamus replied.

"That would be Sir Walter Butler, but are you sure you wish to go in?"

"Of course we are," I replied. "Why wouldn't we be?"

"The town is full of plague. Hundreds of people have died. We only have a few hundred soldiers left to guard the place. Just as well Cromwell doesn't know how depleted we are."

"Cromwell knows a lot more than you give him credit for," Seamus replied. "Tell me, do you have a Captain Tickle located here?"

"Yes, we do. He is one of our Irish officers in charge of two of the gates into Kilkenny. He is securing them against Cromwell."

"Oh, we know exactly what he is up to," Aoife said. "Where would we find him?"

"Why this interest in Captain Tickle?"

"We think he is working with Cromwell to betray the town!" I said.

"Do you indeed?" he replied as he turned to the other soldiers with him. "Sergeant Clarke, arrest these people at once. They are spies!"

"Yes, Captain Tickle!"

"Captain Tickle!" I gasped.

We were immediately surrounded by a group of ten soldiers with swords drawn.

"If anyone of them puts up a fight, execute them immediately!" Captain Tickle ordered.

"Yes, sir!"

"Stand down, Seamus," Phelim whispered as Seamus drew his sword. "This is not the time or place to fight."

Seamus reluctantly handed over his sword and we

were led away by the soldiers.

"Ever get a feeling of déja vu?" I said to Aoife.

"I don't know what that means," Aoife replied. "Though, if you ask me, I feel we've been through this before in Wexford."

I stopped in my tracks and looked at her, unsure whether or not she was making a joke.

"*Why are you stopping?*" one of the soldiers roared. "*Keep up!*"

I jumped in fright and Aoife laughed aloud.

"How can you laugh at a time like this?" I said. "We're going to be locked up again!"

"Don't worry, I've told you before that everything will turn out the way it's supposed to. "

"But how do you know that?"

"I can't tell you yet. Keep trusting me. I promise you the day is drawing closer when everything will become clearer."

"Come on now, no talking!" the solider ordered.

"Where's Ferdia?" I asked, looking around.

"Just like him to skedaddle when the going gets tough!" Seamus declared.

"Keep your wits about you," Phelim whispered. "Ferdia, that old bag of bones, is around somewhere. Listen for my whistle. When he appears, be prepared to run."

We were being led into the centre of the town. As

we walked on we were looked at with curiosity by the Kilkenny people.

"They probably think we are spies!" Seamus glumly muttered. "You know what happens to spies!"

"What happens?" I asked.

"You don't want to know!"

"I do, that's why I asked you!"

"Well, it's not very pleasant."

"Stop that talking!" one of the soldiers demanded.

"I prefer whistling myself," Phelim replied and he let out a loud whistle.

Ferdia suddenly appeared and ran directly into the group of soldiers who were guarding us, tossing two of them up in the air and onto their backs. One of them raised his sword to attack Ferdia.

"Do not harm that horse!" shouted Seamus as he grabbed the sword and cut the belt off the soldier's trousers.

The soldier ran off, holding his trousers as he tried to prevent them falling down around his ankles.

The rest of the soldiers by this time had fled so that left just us and Ferdia in the square.

Phelim grabbed Aoife and almost threw her up onto Ferdia's back. Then it was my turn and he flung me up so violently that I only just saved myself from falling down the other side of the horse.

"Now, dear people," he yelled, *"I suggest we run!"*

Ferdia took off down the narrow streets, Phelim and Seamus running behind us.

At last Aoife drew Ferdia to a halt and let the men catch up.

"Let's double around and try and catch Captain Tickle!" I suggested when they did.

"Just what I was thinking," Seamus said.

"Don't be taking credit for the lad's clever suggestion!" Phelim scoffed.

"Stop arguing, the two of you! Let's get on with it!" Aoife urged.

We made our way back until the gate came in sight. Captain Tickle was still there, laughing and joking with some of his men.

"Look at him!" Seamus cried. "I've a good mind to run him through with this sword!"

"You do, and you'll be shot," I replied. "We need to do this the proper way, through the correct authorities."

"Sir Walter Butler, the Governor of Kilkenny?" Phelim suggested.

"Exactly!" I replied. "He'll probably be around the town somewhere checking the defences."

"We'll need to move quickly," Aoife said. "Liam, get on Ferdia and ride around the town to try and find him."

Seamus gave me a leg-up and then handed me the letter which proved the captain's guilt.

"Take good care of that, Liam – it's the only proof we have," he said. "We'll keep an eye on Captain Tickle in the meantime."

Ferdia took off at speed towards the town.

How will I know the governor when I see him? I wondered. I soon got the answer to my question when we stopped at one of the gates where a large group of men were busy fortifying the entrance. One man was giving orders to the rest.

"Put your backs into it, men – our numbers may be low, but we can still try to put a halt to Cromwell and his army!"

The men were obeying him without question.

"Go on, Ferdia, this could be the person we're looking for," I whispered in his ear.

We drew closer and halted.

"Governor Butler?" I asked.

"Get off your horse when addressing the governor!" a nearby soldier shouted.

"Leave him be, Corporal Kennedy, he's only a boy!" the man laughed. "Yes, son, I am Sir Walter Butler. What can I do for you?"

"If you please, sir, my name is Liam. I have important news about one of your men – Captain Tickle."

"Tickle? What has that scallywag been up to now?"

I showed him the letter. His face darkened as he read the contents.

"Where did you get this letter, Liam?"

"From a reliable source, sir!"

The governor thought for a moment. "Corporal Kennedy!" he called.

"Yes, sir."

"Get the horses. Take two men and come with me. We're going to find Captain Tickle."

"He's at the main gate, sir," I replied.

"Well done, Liam. If the contents of this letter are to be believed you have helped to save a lot of lives today."

Together we rode back to the main gate.

Aoife and Phelim were there, waiting patiently.

Captain Tickle was nowhere to be seen.

"Where is the captain?" I asked.

Aoife pointed over to a spot where Seamus was sitting.

"I can see Seamus sitting there, but where's the captain?" I asked.

"Have a look at what he's sitting on!" said Phelim.

He was sitting on the captain!

"Best way to keep a person in the one place is to sit on them!" he laughed.

As the governor approached, Seamus stood up to let the captain get to his feet.

Tickle stood up and brushed himself down. "You'll pay for this, pirate," he muttered. "Governor Butler, this man has just assaulted me and had the cheek to sit down on me as if I were a cushion or a chair. I demand that he be imprisoned immediately for his insolence."

"Captain Tickle, can you explain this letter?" the governor angrily demanded, as he waved the paper in the air.

As I watched I could see the confidence drain from Tickle as he recognised the paper which was being held up.

"Letter, sir? No. What is it?"

"It's from you, captain!"

"From me, sir? No idea what you're talking about, sir. I haven't been in touch with Cromwell at all, sir – don't believe them!"

"I never mentioned Cromwell to you, captain!"

"It's a forgery, sir, that's what it is!"

"I recognise your handwriting, Tickle! What were you thinking, man?"

"I was trying to save lives, sir!"

"You were trying to save your own blasted neck!" Seamus growled. "We'll soon find out how tough that neck of yours is, now that everyone knows what you've been up to."

"Arrest him immediately!" the governor ordered.

The captain was escorted away, still protesting his innocence.

"We do have an advantage over Cromwell, sir," I then said.

"Really? What is that, young fellow?"

"Cromwell doesn't know that Captain Tickle has been arrested so he will expect him to be here to help him gain entrance to the town."

"He's right, Governor," Phelim said. "Cromwell will be expecting easy access. He won't be prepared for a siege. That will set him back a bit!"

"Just as well," the governor replied. "Troop numbers are low because of the plague, and we are relying on the local people to help defend the town. They will be no match for Cromwell and his army – yet we have been ordered by Ormonde to delay Cromwell as long as we can, to give other towns time to prepare to fight against him. We may hold out for a while but, in the end, surrender is inevitable."

On the 22nd March, Cromwell's army finally approached Kilkenny.

The governor called us to Kilkenny Castle.

"Cromwell has offered us terms of surrender. I thought you deserved to know this first, due to your bravery in exposing the treachery of Captain Tickle."

"Excuse me, sir, what has happened to Captain Tickle?" I asked.

"He has been hanged!"

"Hanged? But why?" I asked, shocked.

The governor looked at me strangely.

Aoife intervened. "Liam, that is the accepted punishment given to those who betray their cause. You cannot change this. It is the age that we live in."

"I salute your concern for your fellow man, Liam," the governor said, "but an example had to be made and, as the young girl says, this is the law. Perhaps one day we will have more humane ways of dealing with traitors, but that is not for you or me to decide today. We have more urgent matters to discuss."

"What terms has Cromwell offered?" Phelim asked.

"He will allow all soldiers and priests to leave safely. Citizens can choose to leave with their possessions or remain here without harm."

"Quite generous terms," Seamus observed.

"I agree," the governor replied. "We'll refuse them, of course. We're not going to make it that easy for him!"

"What do you think he'll do?" I asked.

"I expect an attack, but I think we are well prepared for it. So let's see what the next few days bring."

We did not have long to wait. An attack came the next morning, but it was not successful. A further attack followed and one of the walls was damaged by cannon. At the same time some of Cromwell's forces attacked two different parts of the town. Some were forced back, some gained control of part of the town.

There were losses on both sides.

"We won't last much longer," the governor confided in us, when we met him at the castle again.

"Cromwell has lost people too, sir," Seamus said. "He'll be thinking twice about attacking again so quickly."

"Some of his army already control parts of the town. I can't risk the lives of the townspeople any longer. We will have to surrender."

Just then a message from Cromwell arrived. The governor read the contents.

"He is offering terms of surrender again," he said.

"What will you do?" I asked.

"I shall ask for time to consider the offer."

"With all due respect, Governor, Cromwell may not grant you that time," I said.

The governor looked directly at us.

"You may be right, but we have to try one last time. It is our duty to try and slow down the march of Cromwell, so we can to give other towns a chance to prepare to fight."

"That's if any of the rest of them want to fight," Aoife countered.

The governor sighed wearily. "You may be right but, as long as we have Hugh Dubh O'Neill in Clonmel, we have hope."

"Who is Hugh Dubh O'Neill?" Aoife asked as we left the castle.

"The best Irish leader in the country!" Seamus said as he and Phelim approached us in the street. "He's a clever fella too – Cromwell won't have it easy with him!"

"That remains to be seen," Phelim replied.

The governor was forced to agree to a surrender within days, after another breach in the town wall. He was allowed to leave safely with his men.

"We are allowed one hundred muskets and one hundred pikes to defend ourselves," he told us.

"Defend yourselves against what?" I asked. "Surely the battle is over for you now?"

"Aye, but it's not Cromwell they have to fear now, but those brigands who roam the country robbing folks," Phelim replied, looking at Seamus.

"Those scoundrels have nothing to do with us privateers. We don't rob our own. Not like those Tories!" Seamus protested.

"Tories?" I asked.

"That's what we call them," Phelim said. "A dangerous bunch of robbers and cutthroats for sure."

"How come we haven't met them yet?" I asked.

Phelim put his hand on my shoulder. "Let's hope we don't, Liam, for all our sakes."

As the governor prepared to leave, he called Aoife and me to one side.

"You have performed a great service these last few

months for your people. I have two tasks for you, if you choose to accept."

Aoife and I looked at one another and nodded in agreement.

"I will provide you with some fresh horses. Make your way to Clonmel if you can. Meet with Hugh Dubh O'Neill. Tell him what you have seen. He may be able to figure out a way to stop Cromwell."

"We will, sir," I replied.

"The second task I ask because you and your group have proved yourselves to be most trustworthy. I want you to deliver a sum of money to Cromwell."

"Money?" I asked.

"Yes. He insists that the town pay two thousand pounds to his army to stop them from looting the town. It is in this satchel here. Will you and your friends take it?"

The bag was handed to me. "Of course we will, sir."

"Good lad. That's a lot of money, but I know you are the right people to hand it over. Make sure it goes to Cromwell directly."

We walked out of the town with the governor and his troops. As Cromwell had promised, they were allowed to leave peacefully.

We made our way to Cromwell's camp where our way was blocked by one of his units.

"We have direct business with his Excellency

Cromwell!" I declared. I was shaking and nervous, but I tried not to show it.

"Isn't he the brave one!" one of the soldiers laughed.

"Let the boy through!" bellowed a voice.

It was Cromwell, looking much better than the last time we saw him. He was dressed in full armour and had a red sash tied around his waist.

"What business does a young Irish boy and his companions have here?" he asked as he pointed the baton he was holding in his hand at us.

"I bring the money from Governor Butler, sir. He said to give it to you directly."

"He must trust you very much to hand over such a large sum."

"Yes sir, I suppose he does," I replied.

"Your face looks familiar – have we met before?"

"Yes, sir, at Drogheda."

"The boy and the girl in the stable – yes, I remember. I think I saw you at Wexford as well, did I not?"

"Yes, sir."

"I was not at my best then."

"No, you had malaria, sir."

"Did I indeed? You seem to be very well informed. Are you a spy?"

"No, sir!"

"Fear not, boy. You are not in danger here. You have

my word. Where is your family?"

"They are my family, sir," I said pointing to Aoife, Seamus, Phelim and Ferdia.

"I mean, where are your parents, boy?"

I found I couldn't answer. I had no memory of them. "I don't know, sir," I said then. "I'm trying to find them."

"I have children of my own, and I know I miss them greatly when I do not see them. I am sure that your parents are missing you. I hope you find them."

"When will you see your family again?" I asked.

"The English parliament has been writing to me since January, asking me to return to help deal with some Scottish rebels. I shall probably return shortly and see them again then."

"When do you expect to return?"

Cromwell looked at me sharply. "That is too much information for a young lad like you to know. I will not leave until my work in Ireland is done. You and your friends may leave the camp now. My soldiers will not harm you."

"What did he say to you?" Seamus asked as we left the camp. "Was he trying to find out what you know?"

"No. I told him I was looking for my parents. He said he hoped that I found them."

"What? I don't trust that man."

"He seemed sincere."

"Tell that to all the families of the people he has killed," Seamus replied.

"Not to mention all the priests and monks his army killed in cold blood and the abbeys he burned," Phelim added.

I had no answer to that.

"He said that he might be leaving Ireland soon," I said.

"Really?" Seamus replied. "Well, that is news indeed."

"Yes, some trouble with the Scots apparently. But he's not going until he has finished his business here."

"Well, if he is under pressure to return," said Phelim, "maybe if someone can slow him down he may be forced to leave before his mission is complete."

"Then let's make our way to Clonmel," Aoife piped up, "and carry out the governor's last request to speak to Hugh Dubh O'Neill!"

"Why not?" Seamus replied. "Might as well be hung for a sheep as a lamb."

"I don't get that?" I said.

"Not so clever then after all, are you, Master Liam?" he laughed.

Chapter 7

Clonmel, 1650

"**W**hat do we know about Hugh Dubh O'Neill?" Aoife asked as we rode along the road to Clonmel.

"I know a thing or two about him," I said. "He was born in Brussels and his uncle was the great Owen Roe O'Neill. He has fought in the Spanish army, so he should know a thing or two about battles. He's been in Clonmel since February, getting the town ready to defend itself against Cromwell's army."

"How do you know that?" Aoife asked.

Phelim and Seamus looked at one another and grinned.

"*School project!*" they both said at the same time.

When we arrived at the town we saw some of Cromwell's forces camped outside.

"How will we get in?" I asked.

"We'll go quietly around the outside, looking for a way in," Phelim suggested. "Cromwell's main army isn't here yet, so there may be a gap in their forces somewhere."

We got off our horses and took off their saddles and hid them. After taking our saddlebags, we let them go free so that we would not draw attention to ourselves. Ferdia stayed with us. As we walked we realised that the town was protected on three sides by tall thick walls. The other side was protected by the River Suir. We walked along the river, wondering if there was a bridge to get across to the town.

Suddenly Ferdia took off.

"Where's he going?" I asked as he galloped away into the distance.

"He's a very private creature," Phelim replied. "He likes his free time!"

"I'm not surprised!" Seamus mocked. "Who wouldn't want some free time after being stuck with you for so long!"

As luck would have it, we found a small boat on the banks of the River Suir and rowed across. Then we walked again until we came to a town entrance.

As we entered the town Phelim stopped by a bearded individual who was busy giving orders to a bunch of soldiers.

"Don't listen to him, lads, he doesn't know what he's doing!" Phelim joked.

"Well, Phelim, I didn't expect to see you here!" the man proclaimed. "Who are these friends with you?"

"This is Seamus – a, eh, privateer – Aoife and Liam."

"It's a pleasure to meet you all," he replied.

"The pleasure is ours, sir!" I said, feeling proud of coming up with this polite answer.

"Sir! No need to call me *sir*, young lad – call me Hugh!"

My eyes opened wide. "You're Hugh Dubh O'Neill?"

"You've heard of me?"

"Well, Seamus says if anyone can stop Cromwell, it's you!"

Seamus blushed slightly. "I may have said some words to that effect."

Hugh laughed. "I hope you're right!"

"How many soldiers do you have?" Phelim asked.

"I arrived last December with 1200 soldiers from Ulster. We've lost some through plague, but we've gathered up some extra help from the soldiers who were fighting at Cashel and Kilkenny. We don't have much food left, but we plan to hold on until reinforcements arrive."

"Are you sure help will come?" I asked.

"We're hoping to get more soldiers from Ulster to help."

"That's very optimistic of you!" Seamus observed.

Hugh laughed. "A cynical pirate! Why am I not surprised?"

"Always expect the worst!" he replied. "And we're *privateers* not *pirates!*"

"Of course you are!"

Cromwell's main forces arrived within days. The date was the 27th April 1650.

"There's over 8000 soldiers out there," Phelim said as he looked down from the town wall over the surrounding area.

"He'll start shelling the place soon, I expect," Seamus said.

"Not with those guns he has," I said, pointing towards the banks where the artillery was settled. "They are smaller than the ones he had in Drogheda and Wexford. He'll need bigger ones!"

During the day the soldiers fired on the town but without any lasting damage.

"Looks like you were right about those guns," Aoife said. "School Project?"

"Yup!" I laughed.

"We're off on a skirmish to upset Cromwell's soldiers outside. Who's up for a challenge?" Hugh asked as he approached us.

"No thanks, I've had enough excitement for a lifetime," Phelim replied.

"I'll never turn down the chance to box a few English ears," Seamus said.

"Count me in, sir!" I cried.

"All right, lad, you're in," he laughed.

"I don't have any weapon," I said.

"You won't need one, lad – we're not out for killing today. We just want to upset them a little."

"Like putting a stick in a hornet's nest?" Aoife inquired.

"Something like that! It takes our soldiers' minds off what's happening, and it gives them a good laugh. Plus, and this is the really good part, Cromwell hates it!"

"Well, I'm going with you!" Aoife declared. "If Liam goes, so do I!"

"I won't stop you!" Hugh replied. "It must be great to have a friend who cares for you so much, Liam."

I paused for a moment. I had never thought of this before. "Yes, yes, it is," I replied. "She watches out for me, and I for her."

"That's how it should be. Meet me here this evening. We'll go out when it's dark."

That evening we gathered with the soldiers at one of the town gates.

Hugh began to speak. "Right! Now, gentlemen!"

Aoife coughed loudly.

"I beg your pardon, Aoife! Right! Now, lady and gentlemen, here's the plan. We are going out from these walls tonight to disturb the soldiers who are busy getting the area ready for a siege. They are making ladders to scale the walls and building frames that will carry their heavy guns that are due to arrive any day now. We want to destroy these if we can and cause as much havoc as possible."

"How do we do that, sir?" I asked.

"We need to save ammunition and do this as quietly as we can. So good old Mother Nature is going to help us. Bring in the sacks, lads!"

A number of soldiers came forward with some foul-smelling bags.

"Ugh! What's that?" Aoife asked.

"The best cow dung this part of the country!" Hugh proudly declared. "A few shovels of this in the right places will scatter those forces for a while.

I sniffed it. "That smells revolting!"

"Take a bag between two of you. You haven't seen anything yet!" Hugh laughed. "Bring up the secret weapon!"

A soldier brought up another bag except this time there seemed to be something alive in it.

"What is that?" I asked.

The soldier opened the top of the bag so we could see what was in it.

The head of an animal with black and white stripes appeared.

"By the heavens, what is that?" Seamus asked.

"It's a skunk!" I said.

"I've heard about them! Keep it away from me!" Seamus roared.

"An explorer friend of mine brought it back from the Americas," said Hugh. "The poor soldiers won't know what hit them!"

We left the town silently and made our way down to a bunch of Cromwell's soldiers who were lying asleep while one soldier stood guard.

The soldiers had taken their boots off and had left them beside them as they slept.

We split into small groups and walked gently around the camp so as not to disturb the sentry. We shovelled the dung into the shoes of the sleeping soldiers. When this was all done, Seamus crept close to the sentry, holding the skunk. He waited for a signal from Hugh.

Hugh and his group crawled up to the wooden constructions that had been made to help with the siege and poured oil over them. He lit a match and they were all set alight.

Before the sentry could act, Seamus threw the

skunk right into his face and the poor man ran off into the distance howling. This woke the rest of the soldiers whose first instinct was to put on their boots. We heard the shouts of disgust from them as one by one they discovered what was in their footwear.

"Put that fire out!" one shouted.

"But what about our boots?"

"Never mind the boots – put that fire out!"

The soldiers were forced to run around in their bare feet. *"Ouch!"* they cried as they ran on the hard ground.

We got safely back into the town before we were discovered. We looked and laughed at the chaos outside.

"It won't stop them, but it will slow them down!" Hugh laughed.

These skirmishes continued over the next few weeks. We continued to hit them when they least expected it, one time just before dawn.

But eventually the large guns arrived and blew a hole in the wall that could be accessed by Cromwell and his army.

"Well, that's it, I suppose," Phelim remarked. "They'll come in through that hole, fight their way into the town and open one of the gates. Once the gates are open Cromwell and his cavalry will be in to cut us all to shreds."

"You're a very calm one, considering what you have just said," Seamus said.

"No point in grumbling about it," Phelim shrugged.

"*Nonsense!*" Hugh shouted. "I have planned for this very event. This is exactly what I expected Cromwell to do. We're not beaten yet. I want every man, woman and child down to that wall breach at once!"

Aoife and I joined the crowd and we ran down to the damaged wall.

"We're going to stop the soldiers getting in!" Hugh shouted.

"We can't rebuild the wall!" Aoife said.

"Who said anything about rebuilding the wall! We're going to build something inside the wall! They'll have no idea what hit them!"

"There's no time! Cromwell is probably on his way with his soldiers now!" one of the soldiers said.

"I don't think so. Cromwell won't send his soldiers in today. He'll wait until morning," I said.

"How do you know that, young fella?" Hugh said, looking at me curiously.

"He's been right about everything so far," Phelim told him.

"How come?"

"Never mind!" said Phelim. "But he is!"

"Well, in this case I agree with him! We'll have time

enough to prepare a surprise they won't forget!" Hugh declared.

We were broken up into small groups. Some had to fetch earth and clay to build up small mounds and hills. Hugh ordered us to create two long walls of earth and timber which came together in a V-shape at the end. The walls were about two metres high and at least fifty metres long, I reckoned. Soldiers and two cannon were put at the top of the V and the cannon were loaded with chain-shot. I was interested to see that these 'chain-shot' were half-balls chained together which would tumble through the air when fired.

I looked at the makeshift wall with admiration after we had finished putting it together.

"This is a very clever idea, sir," I replied.

"That's if it works," Phelim grumbled.

"Ah, have you deduced how it will stop the solders getting in?" Hugh asked.

"Yes," I replied. "Cromwell's men will flood through the gap and be caught in the V where they will be fired on by the soldiers with the cannon."

"Absolutely right, Liam. They won't know what's hit them until it's too late!"

The next morning, the soldiers attacked as expected

and flooded through the breach in the wall. As they neared the top of the V, they were blasted by the chainshot from the cannon. They had no idea what was happening. Hundreds and hundreds rushed through the breach in the wall and were killed. They were not able to retreat because of the pressure of numbers trying to force themselves through the gap in the wall behind them. More and more came through the gap. It was a slaughter. They never had a chance. Those who survived the cannon were killed by O'Neill's soldiers and townsmen who went in with muskets, swords, pikes, scythes and stones to finish them off.

By the time it was over almost a thousand soldiers lay dead or dying.

"Those poor men!" I said.

"They would have shown no mercy to you or Aoife, remember that," Seamus responded.

"Remember, Liam, you cannot change any of this," Aoife whispered. "You are here to witness what is happening and remember so that you can tell others."

"What will happen now?" I asked.

"They'll probably charge again once they realise what has happened," Hugh replied.

"Cromwell will have some task trying to persuade them to get back in there!" Seamus laughed.

"That was the infantry who made the first attempt. I don't think they'll come back for more," Phelim said.

He was right. Later on, the cavalry tried to force their way through the gap on foot. They were known as 'Ironsides' because they were so tough and they forced us all back into the town, but they could not defeat Hugh's troops. After some hours they finally withdrew, leaving many more dead or badly injured.

The townsfolk of Clonmel cheered when they saw the soldiers retreating.

"It's not many that get to defeat the great Cromwell in battle," Phelim remarked.

"It cannot last," Hugh replied. "We have very little food left, and I don't think we are going to get any extra troops."

"What are you going to do?" I asked.

"Live to fight another day of course!" he laughed. "We will sneak out while it is dark and make our way to Waterford."

Hugh met with the mayor of the town, John White, to let him know of his plans and give him the opportunity to negotiate a surrender.

"Cromwell will be very angry when he finds out you are gone," the mayor said.

"Don't tell him!" I suggested.

"What?" the mayor replied.

"Cromwell is looking for Hugh Dubh O'Neill, the only Irish commander to inflict huge losses on his army. I think he will be happy to offer a truce in the hope of capturing him. Go out there and negotiate this, but don't tell him Hugh is gone!"

"Liam is right. I think it could work!" Seamus said.

"It's certainly worth a try," the mayor and Hugh agreed.

That night Hugh and his soldiers left the town quietly.

Mayor White offered to surrender the town to Cromwell if he would guarantee the people and their property would not be harmed. Cromwell agreed.

"Why did Cromwell agree?" Aoife asked.

"He has lost enough soldiers in battle," Phelim replied. "He wants to win without further loss."

Later that day Cromwell rode in with his cavalry and met the mayor.

"Bring me Hugh O'Neill and his followers!" he demanded.

"I'm very sorry, Excellency, but those men have left the town!"

Cromwell's face went red with anger.

"Gone, you say! Gone where?"

"I don't know, sir."

"This was not part of the surrender agreement! Why didn't you tell me?"

"Well, you never asked, sir. If you had asked we would have told you!"

Cromwell grew angrier still.

"I have lost thousands of good men here in Clonmel because of that man!"

The mayor spoke up. "Your Excellency has a reputation for sticking to his word when he agrees to a surrender."

Cromwell sighed and looked over at us.

He steered his horse in our direction.

"You children again! Why do you follow me so? What are you? Some kind of evil spirits?"

"Oh no, sir!" Aoife replied. "We just have a keen interest in the pursuits of a great general such as yourself."

Cromwell sniffed. "Well then, no matter. I don't suppose you know where that renegade O'Neill is?"

"Us? No, no idea at all. How would we know anything like that?" Seamus replied.

"You are fortunate that I have guaranteed the safety of the people in this town. I will not break that promise. Rest assured we will find your local hero and his ragtag army. Where did O'Neill get his military experience?"

"He served with an Irish unit in the Spanish Army, Your Excellency," I said.

"Blast you and your overseas companions, O'Neill! I will track you down and destroy you!"

He called one of his officers over.

"Ride on towards Waterford with a large number. O'Neill is probably headed there for support. Catch

128

him alive if you can. If not, you may be able to pick off some of his soldiers."

The officer saluted and left to carry out his mission.

Cromwell turned back to us. "I must return to England soon. Will you follow me there also?" he asked.

"I don't think the English air would agree with us!" Seamus replied sarcastically.

"Oh no, sir!" Aoife replied. "We will stay in Ireland."

"I count my blessings for that!" he said and rode away. *"To Waterford, men! It is a town that will soon bow to our English superiority!"*

His men cheered.

As they left the town we heard the familiar neighing of a horse. Ferdia! The other horses we had left outside earlier were with him too. He led them over to us.

"Where have you been, boy?" I asked as I stroked his mane.

"Up to no good, I expect!" Phelim laughed. "Trust him to turn up when the danger is over!"

Ferdia nuzzled me.

"I think he wants you to go somewhere with him," Phelim said.

"Go where?" I asked. "Can't we just stay here for a while? I just want to close my eyes and sleep for a long, long time."

"You can't!" Aoife replied.

"What do you mean?"

"You have to keep on the move. You can't give up now!"

"I'm not talking about giving up! But what do you mean I have to keep on the move?"

"Remember that bright light you said you could see that seemed to be getting farther away each time? Have you seen it recently?"

"Well, now that you mention it, I haven't seen it."

"That's because *you* are getting farther away from *it* – you have to find it!"

"What are you talking about? How am I going to find it?"

Ferdia nudged me again.

"Look!" Aoife said as she pointed at the horse. "Ferdia is going to help you."

"But what about the rest of you?"

"Oh, don't worry, we're coming too!" Aoife said.

"Where are we going?"

Phelim helped me onto Ferdia. He had retrieved the saddles for the other horses which the others now mounted.

"I think we're following in Cromwell's tracks," I said, as Ferdia led the way.

"Then we're on our way back to Waterford," Phelim said as he trotted up beside us.

"I don't think he will find any more success there than he did last time," I said.

We travelled at a steady pace and stopped for the night in a wooded area.

"You sleep, Liam – I will watch over you," Aoife said as she tucked me in under a blanket. "Can you see the bright light anywhere in the night sky?"

I looked up into the sky for a few minutes. I finally located it and pointed upwards.

"Yes! There it is. I can just about see it. It's very faint. Do you see it?"

"Yes, I do. You must follow it, Liam, *you must*."

"You keep saying that, but why?"

"That is your way out of this. You do not belong here!"

"What do you mean?"

"I cannot tell for certain how, I just feel it."

"What about you then?"

"What do you mean?"

"Do you belong here?"

"I can't answer that, I don't know. Now sleep, I will watch over you."

Aoife put her hand on my head and stroked my forehead. My eyes grew heavy. Just as I was about to fall asleep I heard a woman's voice calling to me again. I had not heard her voice for some time. It was very comforting.

"It's all right, Liam, I'm here. You're going to come back to me. Come back, Liam! Come back!"

Then everything went dark and I fell asleep.

Chapter 8

Waterford and Youghal, 1650

When we just a few miles outside Waterford we saw a small band of armed men approaching us in the distance.

"I don't like this," Phelim said.

"Tories!" said Seamus. "I'd recognise a bunch of robbers and cut-throats anywhere!"

I looked at him.

"Not that I'd know much about robbing and unpleasant things like that!"

"As you're the expert, how do you suggest we handle this?" Phelim asked.

"Do what every good bandit does when in trouble. Run away!"

We turned our horses around and rode hard in the opposite direction.

The Tories started to chase us. As they gained ground one of them fired a musket at us.

"They're shooting at us!" Aoife shouted.

"A warning shot only! If they wanted us dead, we would be dead!" Seamus replied. *"Besides, they want to see what we have before they kill us!"*

"I don't like the sound of that!" I shouted. As I spoke I could hear a bullet fly past my ear.

"They're catching up on us!" Aoife cried in alarm.

"That's not the worst part!" Phelim replied. *"Look up ahead!"*

Another group of armed men were directly in our path.

"We're done for!" Seamus said. *"Trapped on both sides!"*

It was too late to slow down now.

But, as we got closer, we saw a recognisable figure amongst the group. It was Hugh Dubh O'Neill!

We rode up to them.

"Having some trouble?" he joked.

"Just a little!" I replied.

Hugh addressed his men.

"I think those other riders need some friendly persuasion."

His men rode off in pursuit of the Tories who turned tail and fled as soon as they saw them approach.

"We thought you would be inside Waterford now, Hugh, safe and sound!" I said, once I got my breath back.

"Governor Preston wouldn't let us in. He said there wasn't enough food to spare. So we have separated into smaller groups to avoid Cromwell. I've told most of my soldiers to try to get back to Ulster."

"What will you do now?" I asked.

"I'm not finished with the fighting yet. I'll go to Limerick to see what help I can provide."

"God help the English when they come up against you again!" Seamus declared.

"You're the last man they'll want to see!" I added.

"I'm counting on it!" he laughed, and he rode off. "*Stay safe!*" he shouted back to us.

"You seemed a bit worried back there, Seamus," Phelim joked.

"I was just trying to distract the children. I knew we were safe all the time!" Seamus replied.

Aoife and I laughed.

We arrived at Waterford to find Cromwell's troops once again starting to set up camp outside. The town was still refusing to surrender.

"Cromwell is leaving!" Seamus said one day after he

had returned from a spying mission in Cromwell's camp. "He's going to Youghal."

"He already controls that town," I said.

"It's flight not fight! He is sailing back to England. The English Parliament is insisting that he return. They are afraid of an attack from Scotland."

"What will happen here?" Aoife asked.

"His second-in-command Henry Ireton will continue the campaign here," I said.

"There won't be any tears shed when Cromwell leaves," Phelim said.

"We should go to Youghal," Aoife replied.

"Yes, I'd love to watch the scoundrel leave these shores," Seamus said. "Let's go!"

Ferdia whinnied as if in agreement.

"Well, I must say I would very much like to see the back of the scoundrel, so I'm up for it," Phelim agreed. "One last trip, why not?"

When we arrived in Youghal, the finishing touches were being put to the ship that Cromwell was to board to take him back to England.

As he travelled through the town to make his way to the quays he was cheered by the people.

"He'll be a hero when he gets back to England,"

Seamus said. "The man who defeated the Irish on their own turf."

"He had the biggest army and the best weapons the country has ever seen, so how could he lose!" Phelim replied. "And he has been ruthless."

"His name will be cursed by generations in Ireland to come, that's for sure," Seamus said.

We followed Cromwell down to the quays where there was a reception waiting to see him off. When this was complete he boarded the ship. Then he turned around to look at the crowd. As he looked at the various faces I felt his eyes settle on me.

Cromwell spoke to an aide on the ship who then disembarked and approached our group. He looked at me.

"His Excellency requires your presence."

"What does he want me for?" I asked.

"His Excellency did not say. He said to say this is not an order, but a request. You are free to refuse."

"Don't trust him!" Seamus warned.

"Go speak to him," Aoife suggested.

"I'll go with you, lad," Seamus said as he put his hand on his sword.

"It's all right, Seamus – something tells me he's not going to harm me."

"If you will come this way," the aide said as he turned to walk back.

I accompanied him to the ship.

I climbed onto the deck and walked up to Cromwell.

"I had a feeling you would be here today before I left."

"What made you think that, sir?"

"Ever since Drogheda you have been with me on my travels. I feel we are kindred spirits in a way. I have had my own particular journey and you have had yours."

"I don't understand."

"I know why I am here. I believe in the Puritan way of life. I disagree with the excesses and extravagances of the Catholic Church. I am here to uphold English rule of law on a Catholic people who have turned their back on accepted practices."

"Accepted English practices," I said.

"That may be the case, but the law is the law. You can argue the rights and wrongs of it, but I serve the will of the English Parliament which ultimately rules this island of yours."

"Does this justify the killing of thousands throughout the country?"

"I do not make up the rules of warfare. Where towns have surrendered peacefully there have been no killings and no damage to property."

"What about the towns like Drogheda and Wexford

that did not surrender?"

"I offered them a peaceful surrender. They declined. They had to pay the price. What I have done is no worse than what any of your other leaders over the years."

"That's not what the people say."

"What do they say?"

"That you are the most hated man in Irish history."

"That may well be the case. All I ask of you is to check all your facts before you judge me."

"Why does that matter to you?"

"I am just a simple English country squire who has grown to lead this army which has wreaked devastation across your country. I do not force any man or woman to convert to my religion. What they do in their own time is a matter for themselves and their God. I believe I am acting under the will of God. It is God's will that you be subjected to English rule."

"How can you be sure of that?"

"Because we are victorious! My army behaves very differently to your Irish armies, you know. I do not allow them to steal and rob from the population. I insist that they behave and pay the local people for whatever food and services they provide. Some of the Irish armies we have been fighting have lots of English Royalist soldiers who are more interested in restoring the king to England than the rights of the Irish people.

They are well known for burning and looting towns they have taken over. Are we really worse than they are?"

"*All aboard!*" came a shout.

"We are setting sail. You should get off the ship. My journey here is over. My son-in-law Henry Ireton will continue to lead the army in my absence. I have no doubt that he will succeed in conquering the whole island. I hope you come to your journey's end soon."

"Goodbye, sir," I said. "I will never forget you." Nor will the Irish for centuries to come, I thought with a heavy heart.

As I left the ship Cromwell called down to me.

"Remember, Liam, the truth is never black and white! In England they will greet me as a hero. Here, as you say, the people hate me. Seek out the facts for yourself and make up your own mind."

I made my way back to the group.

"What did he say?" Aoife asked.

"He told me to check the facts before I make judgements about him."

"Facts, did you say?" Seamus snorted. "How about the many thousands who have perished at the hands of him and his soldiers! His name will forever be a cursed one in this land!"

We watched the ship sail away and disappear over the horizon.

Then it suddenly grew very dark.

"Come on," Phelim said. "Night is falling, we need to be on our way."

"Where are we going now?" I asked.

"Home," Aoife said. "We are going home."

Where is home? I wondered.

"Well, I will take my leave from you here," Seamus said. "My ship and crew are here in Youghal and there are many more English ships out there which require our attention!"

"Your attention?" I asked.

"Of a *privateering* sort!" he laughed as he gave Aoife and me a hug. "Goodbye all, until we meet again!"

"He won't be missed!" Phelim joked as Seamus left. "I too must get back to Dublin. There is a lot of business there I have to attend to."

"Are you going back on Ferdia?" I asked as he shook my hand and hugged Aoife.

"No, he'll stay with you. When you're finished with him, send him off. He knows his way back. Good luck to you both."

"It's been a great adventure," I started to say but as I looked around Phelim had vanished from sight.

Not only that but the town had disappeared too.

It was just Aoife, Ferdia and I, standing in darkness.

"What's wrong, Liam?" Aoife asked in alarm.

"Everything is vanishing. It's gone very dark!"

"Quick! Can you see the bright light in the sky now?"

"No, it's all dark I told you! Aoife, what's happening?"

"Try to find the light, Liam. Concentrate!"

"I can't! It's not there! No, wait a minute, I see a faint light in the distance! It's getting dimmer!"

"Jump on Ferdia – he will take us to it – hurry, before it's gone!"

We jumped on and Ferdia galloped through the darkness towards the faint light.

"There, up ahead!" I shouted pointing to an area just ahead of us. "It seems to be just hanging there. What is it?"

Ferdia brought us right beside it. It was very dim by now.

"Where is the light coming from?" I wondered.

"Step into it, Liam."

"What?"

"You must step into it!"

"What about you, Aoife?"

"Trust me, Liam. I know you must do this! Hurry – before it disappears completely! Then it will be too late!"

Ferdia pushed me towards the light.

I thought I could hear voices coming from it.

"I don't want to leave you, Aoife!"

"We will meet again!"

"You promise?"

"I promise! Now go, before the light disappears."

I stepped towards the light then ran back for a moment to hug Ferdia's neck and give Aoife a big squeeze.

"Quickly, Liam, go!"

Chapter 9

Present Day

I stepped in and was surrounded by white light and some vague voices.

Suddenly the voices were much clearer. I could hear machines and beeping sounds!

"We're losing him!"

"I can't get a heartbeat!"

"Start the CPR now!"

"It's too late!"

"It's not working!"

"There's no pulse!"

"I said keep doing it!"

My eyes suddenly opened, and I was in a room surrounded by doctors and nurses.

"We have a pulse!" someone shouted. "His heart rate is increasing!"

"Blood pressure stabilising!"

"Breathing normal."

"He's coming back to us!"

"Oh, Liam!" said a voice I recognised.

"Mum?" I murmured before everything went dark again.

I woke up later and looked around to find myself in a hospital ward.

Mum was sitting by my bedside. Her eyes were red. I think she had been crying.

"Hello there, my love," she whispered.

"Mum, what happened?"

A doctor standing beside Mum asked me some questions.

"Do you know where you are, Liam?" he asked.

"I don't know. Some sort of hospital?"

"That's right. Do you remember anything about the accident?"

I rubbed my head, trying to remember.

"I think it was the re-enactment. I got hit on the head."

"Do you remember the cannon?" the doctor asked.

"Cannon?"

Mum said: "A cannon that had been tied securely up on the mound became loose and rolled down the hill towards you and your friends. You pushed them out of the way and Mr Rafferty just managed to prevent you from being crushed, bless him – but you got a nasty bang on the head off the rim of the cannon and were knocked unconscious."

"How long have I been like this?"

"Six days."

"Six days? Not nine months and seventeen days?"

"Nine months and seventeen days?"

"The length of time Cromwell spent in Ireland."

Mum looked at the doctor. She had a worried look on her face.

"Give him time," the doctor suggested calmly. "He's still trying to remember things and make sense of his situation."

"Yes, yes, of course," Mum said.

"You had us worried for a time there," the doctor said.

Mum held my hand tightly. "But we never stopped believing that you would come back to us!"

"You should rest now, Liam," the doctor said. "I'll check up on you later."

"Thanks, Ferdia," Mum said. "We'll see you later."

"Ferdia?" I asked.

"Yes," the doctor laughed. "Everyone calls me Ferdia here!"

"Why?"

"Well, I'm Dr Christian Pferd, so the staff call me Ferdia after the famous Irish legendary warrior – you know, the foster-brother of the great Cúchulainn?"

"Any horses in your background?" I asked.

"Horses?" Mum asked.

Dr Pferd looked at me with a smile. "No horses, apart from my name!"

"Your name?"

"Yes, 'pferd' is the German word for horse, but I wouldn't expect you to know that. See you later!"

"Thanks, doctor," said Mum. "Lie back, darling. You should try and sleep. I'll be here when you wake up, I promise."

I lay back on the pillow and thought about what the doctor had just told me. After a few minutes I closed my eyes.

"He should recover his strength in a few days. He may need to take it easy for a week or two, but he should be fine," I heard Dr Pferd tell Mum.

"Thank you, Ferdia – I don't know what we would have done without you."

"A lot of it is down to him. There's only so much modern medicines can do. We helped him physically to recover, and he had that high fever, but it was his own strong mental state that helped him to come out of the coma and recover."

"I'm glad I made it back safely," I whispered.

"So am I, my darling," I heard Mum say as I drifted off to sleep.

The following day Mr Rafferty came in to see me. His ear was bandaged, and his arm was in a sling.

"Hello, Liam!" he said as he sat down beside the bed. "I'm delighted to see that you're feeling better."

"Are you all right?" I asked.

"I'm fine," he said. "A broken arm and an ear injury from the incident. It'll take more than the Curse of Cromwell to put me out of action!"

"You saved me from the cannon. Thank you. Does the arm hurt?"

"Not at all! I'll be back on the bus before long, then it'll be plain sailing all the way!"

Mr Clarke came in at that point and sat on my other side.

"Hello, Liam. How are you feeling?"

"A lot better, sir, thanks."

"I'm here too!" Mr Rafferty declared.

"Hello, Seamus, it's good to see you up and about – I hope I'm not interrupting!"

"No, Phelim, I wouldn't let you interrupt anything I was doing! No wooden leg today, I see."

"What? Oh yes, I get it! My brief military career – no, no, wooden leg today!" Mr Clarke said with a laugh.

"Seamus? Phelim?" I gasped. "Why are you using those names?"

The two men stared at me.

"Because they're our names, of course!" said Mr Rafferty. "Though I agree that Phelim is a stupid name and he should get rid of it!"

"Can you believe that someone called Seamus is mocking *my* name, Liam?" said Mr Clarke.

I burst out laughing. "Hey, do you two never stop arguing with one another?"

The men looked at one another and then looked at me.

"I don't argue," Seamus asserted.

"Well, I certainly don't argue either!" Phelim countered.

The dispute was interrupted by the arrival of one of the nurses to check my temperature, but they started up with another argument as soon as she left.

A few days later my best mates from school were allowed to visit. They were brought in by Mr Clarke – Phelim.

"Here lies the fallen hero now! You saved our lives!" Pat proclaimed. "You are so lucky – no homework!"

"You are so stupid, Pat!" Nuala said as she pinched his arm.

"*Ow!* What was that for!" he asked, rubbing his arm.

"The last thing on Liam's mind now is homework!"

Mikhail spoke up. "Here, Liam, the whole class made you this *Get Well Soon* card."

"I drew the picture of Cromwell on the front!" Sanjay said.

"It's great!" I said.

They watched, grinning, as I read the messages of goodwill.

I looked up and smiled. "Thanks, guys! I'm feeling a lot better already!"

"Right – we'll leave you now, Liam – we don't want to tire you out," Mr Clarke said. "Come along, you lot! Let's go."

The others got up reluctantly.

"Well, I'm glad you're feeling better, Liam," said Mr Clarke.

"Thank you, Phelim!" I said.

Mikhail laughed. "*Phelim!*" he sniggered.

Nuala pinched him.

"*Ouch!*" he roared. "Why did you do that again?"

"Because you have no sense! Come on now, let's give Liam some rest."

"Mr Clarke – I mean Phelim!" I called as they all started to leave.

"Yes, what is it, Liam?"

"When I get out of here could we have a chat about Oliver Cromwell?"

"Why of course, any time you like! Why do you ask?"

"I just want to check a few things out about him. He was responsible for a lot of deaths in Ireland – but was he as bad as people said he was?"

"Why are you still asking about Cromwell? You must still be concussed!" Pat said. "*Ow!*" he shouted as Nuala gave him a pinch on the arm again. "What are you – the Pinch Grinch? Why do you keep doing that?"

"Because you keep saying stupid things!" she replied.

"You ask a very interesting question, Liam," Mr Clarke said. "Cromwell certainly had a huge impact on this island. His 1652 Act of Settlement punished the Irish Catholics and anyone who supported the king or his son. Many lost their land and had to move to the West of Ireland – to Connacht behind the River Shannon. It is said that Cromwell himself told the Irish they could go 'To Hell or to Connacht' although there is no definitive proof that he ever said this."

"That's a conversation for another day, sir," Nuala suggested.

"Well said, Nuala!" Mr Clarke agreed.

"Information is power, sir!" Pat said.

"As long as it's in the right hands!" Nuala added.

"But I'm left-handed!" Pat joked.

Everybody groaned.

Phelim walked to the door. "All right, folks – it's time to go now."

Soon after they left, Mum came in.

"Mum!"

"Hello, love!"

As usual, she bent over the bed to kiss me – and suddenly froze.

She gasped, straightened up again and put her hand on her stomach.

"Mum, are you all right?"

"The baby's coming!"

I rang the bell for the nurse who came in without delay.

"It's my mum – the baby, the baby!" I spluttered.

She put her arm around Mum. "You come with me, love," she said to her. "Don't worry, Liam, everything will be okay. Professor Kelly is here today. He'll take good care of your mum."

She helped Mum out of the room.

For the next few hours I kept calling the nurses and asking for an update on what was going on. They told me everything was going fine but didn't say much else.

So I worried.

I couldn't sleep, I tossed and turned. The night wore on and at last I fell asleep.

Early the next morning, Dr Pferd himself came in to see me. He was pushing a wheelchair.

"Why don't you hop into this and I'll wheel you in to see your mother?" he suggested.

"Is everything okay?" I asked.

"Of course. Come and see for yourself! I've spoken to Professor Kelly and everything went very well."

"Have you known Professor Kelly for long?"

"Yes, he helped me to train to become a doctor. We call him Captain Kelly because he used to be in the army once upon a time!"

I looked at him in amazement as he helped me out of the bed and into the wheelchair.

He wheeled me along to the maternity section.

When we arrived at my mother's bedside, I heard a whistle. It was the ringtone on Dr Pferd's phone.

"*Oops!* When it whistles, I come running!" he joked as he took it out of his pocket and checked it. "I'll leave you with your mother – congrats again, Geraldine! Emergency! Must run!" And with that he galloped off.

"Sure you must, Ferdia," I muttered to myself as he disappeared.

Mum was lying in the bed. She looked exhausted but happy. Something small wrapped in a yellow blanket was lying beside her.

"Hi, Liam. Someone special wants to say hello."

"The baby… oh my goodness!" I blurted. "Did you … did it … is it okay … are you okay?"

"Everything is fine! Would you like to hold her?"

"Her?"

"Yes, meet your new baby sister!" She put the baby into my arms.

"She's so tiny!"

"Let her rest in the crook of your elbow – give her head support, that's it."

I couldn't believe I was holding this little person who was my sister. As I looked at her tiny frame I noticed her eyes. I had seen them before.

"*Aoife!*" I whispered.

"How did you know we were going to call her that?" Mum asked in surprise.

"We've already met!"

"What did you say?"

"Oh nothing! Aoife is a beautiful name."

I took her little hand in mine and kissed her on the cheek.

"You and I are going to be great friends, Aoife. Now it's my turn to take care of you. I will always keep you safe from harm."

And she smiled at me!

"Look, Mum! Did you see?"

"It's probably just wind," Mum said. "They're too young at that age to smile."

"Okay," I replied.

But I knew that face and I knew that smile. It was a smile that would stay with me for the rest of my life. Nothing, not even the might of Oliver Cromwell's New Model Army would ever come between us. This was the beginning of a new adventure for us both.

Who knew what was ahead of us? But as long as Aoife and I had each other, I knew that we could face the future bravely together.

The End

Afterword

When Cromwell left Ireland in May 1650, he handed control of his army over to his son-in-law Henry Ireton. When Ireton died of plague in Limerick in 1651, Edmund Ludlow took charge. By 1653 the English parliamentary forces had defeated all of the main Irish forces. Many Irish died during this time due to the outbreak of disease and famine. Thousands of others were sent to English colonies in North America and the Caribbean. The 1852 Act for the Settlement of Ireland (also known as The Cromwellian Settlement) punished the Catholic landowners by confiscating their land and handing it over to a new Protestant Ascendancy. In some cases, Catholics received land in Connacht in the west of Ireland instead. Recent studies suggest Cromwell was not in favour of forcing Catholics to leave their land.

Historical Notes

1641 Irish Rebellion: Wealthy Catholic landowners rebelled against English Protestant authorities in Ireland in October 1641. Several thousand Protestants were killed in Ulster, and many more were thrown out of their homes, homes which the Catholics argued they never should have had in the first place, as they had received these by force years previously. The English authorities in Dublin reported that there was a widespread massacre of Protestant people where hundreds of thousands were killed. During 1642 other high-ranking Catholics joined the rebellion. King Charles I sent an army to deal with this. It had to withdraw after the outbreak of the English Civil War in October 1642 between the king and the English parliament (who, among other problems, did not want Charles I to have control of the army). When Cromwell arrived in Ireland in 1649 he was very familiar with the stories of the massacres that had taken place in 1641 and, even though some of this information was incorrect, he felt fully justified in seeking justice for those Protestants who had lost their lives 8 years earlier.

Commander Arthur Aston: An English soldier loyal to Charles I, he became Governor of Drogheda in 1648. He was a Catholic and this had been a handicap in his career as Catholics were suspected of being disloyal to the king and opposed to the Protestant Church of England. However, King Charles I was persuaded to trust him, and he became a commander in the Civil War in England. He was made Governor of Oxford in 1643 but lost a leg as a result of a fall from a horse in 1644 and was relieved as governor. In 1648, he joined the Earl of Ormonde, who had recently been made Commander-in-Chief of the Irish Confederates and Royalist forces in Ireland. Aston was killed in Drogheda by Cromwellian soldiers.

Earl of Ormonde: James Butler was an Anglo-Irish statesman and soldier. He was loyal to the king and leader of the combined Irish Confederate Army and English Royalist Army fighting against Cromwell. In the 1650s he lived in exile in Europe with Charles II.

When Charles was restored to the throne in 1660, Ormonde became a major figure in English and Irish politics, holding many high government offices. He became the Marquess of Ormonde and the Duke of Ormonde and was Chancellor of Trinity College Dublin from 1645 until 1688.

First and Second English Civil Wars: These resulted from various disagreements between King Charles I and Parliament. As a member of parliament, Cromwell fought against the king in the First Civil War in 1641. After the Second Civil War began in 1648, the king was eventually captured and tried for treason. Cromwell himself signed the order for his execution. Charles I was beheaded in 1649.

House of Commons: One of the two parts of the English Parliament. It consisted of representatives of all the many boroughs (towns and districts) and shires (counties) of England.

House of Lords: One of the two parts of the English Parliament, it consisted of the bishops, abbots and nobility.

Hugh Dubh O'Neill (Black Hugh): The nephew of Owen Roe O'Neill. He served in the Spanish Army and was the one Irish leader to inflict heavy losses on Cromwell, at Clonmel. He was captured after the Siege of Limerick in 1651 and, although sentenced to death, as a Spanish citizen he was deported to Spain where he rejoined the Spanish Army.

Irish Confederate Army: After the 1641 rebellion, Irish Catholics formed a number of armies to support Charles I, the Catholic religion in Ireland and the laws of Ireland. In 1648 they formed an alliance with the Earl of Ormonde who led the Royalist forces in Ireland. This alliance failed to defeat Cromwell.

Ironside: a member of Oliver Cromwell's cavalry; or his soldiers in general. Also a nickname for Cromwell himself.

Monarchy: a form of government with a monarch (king or queen) at its head.

Owen Roe (Rua) O'Neill (Red Owen): Born in County Armagh, he served in the Spanish Army and became leader of the Ulster Army contingent of the Irish Confederate Army who agreed an alliance with the Earl of Ormonde against Cromwell. His death in 1649 robbed the Irish of one of its most influential leaders.

Parliament: The English Parliament had existed for centuries before the 17th century. It was divided into representatives of the people of England. It was made up of the House of Commons and the House of Lords. It was usually summoned when necessary by the king. Over the centuries, it gradually limited the power of the king which in the end resulted in the English Civil War and the execution of Charles I in 1649. After the monarchy was restored under Charles II, the parliament still was supreme and all other British kings and queens to come had no real power.

Puritans: The Puritans were English Reformed Protestants who wanted to "purify" the Protestant Church of England from what they considered were "Catholic" practices. They believed in a strictly spiritual way of life and emphasised self-discipline and the importance of the Bible.

Musket: An early version of a rifle, this was a gun used by an infantryman. It was heavy, had a long barrel and was fired from the shoulder.

Privateer: Normally a private person or ship that was given licence during a time of war to attack and rob ships belonging to the enemy.

Royalists: The supporters of the king (also called Cavaliers).

Tories: Groups of ex-soldiers who roamed in small groups around the countryside attacking and robbing those they encountered.

Discussion Questions

1. Did you know about Oliver Cromwell before you read this book? What did you think of him?

2. If you had an opinion about him before you read this book, has this view now changed? Why/Why not?

3. What, in your opinion, were his best qualities? What were his worst?

4. Who were the Puritans?

5. Why were the two English Civil Wars fought?

6. Why did Cromwell invade Ireland?

7. Why did some Irish towns and cities surrender without a fight when Cromwell approached? Why did others resist?

8. Do you believe all the towns and cities should have surrendered immediately to Cromwell?

9. Did Cromwell have much support from the Irish people when he arrived? Why do you think this was the case?

10. Why were there both Irish and English forces fighting together against Cromwell in Ireland?

11. What is your impression of Hugh Dubh O'Neill?

12. Why do you think the English believe Cromwell is a great hero while the Irish believe he is a great villain?

13. What does "To Hell or to Connacht" mean? Who said it?

14. Does it surprise you to hear that Cromwell may not have wished to expel Catholics off their land and force them to live in Connacht?

15. Why did they exhume (dig up) Cromwell's body?

16. Have you ever heard of the Curse of Cromwell? What does it mean to you?

17. Do you believe Cromwell is the most hated man in Irish History? Why/Why not?

Timeline

1599 – Oliver Cromwell born in Huntingdon
1620 – marries Elizabeth Bourchier
1621 – son Robert born
1623 – son Oliver born
1624 – daughter Bridget born
1625 – Charles I becomes King of England
1626 – Cromwell's son Richard born
1628 – son Henry born
Cromwell becomes Member of Parliament for Huntingdon
1629 – daughter Elizabeth born
1630 – Cromwell becomes a Puritan
1632 – son James is born but only lives for a few days
1637 – daughter Mary born
1638 – daughter Frances born
1639 – death of son Robert
Charles I becomes King of England

1641 – Irish uprising against Protestants

1642 – First English Civil War begins between Charles I and Parliament

1644 – death of son Oliver

1645 – creation of New Model Army
Cromwell appointed Lieutenant-General in charge of the cavalry

1646 – end of First English Civil war after Charles I surrenders

1647 – Second English Civil War begins after Charles I gets support from Scotland

1648 – end of Second Civil War; Charles I defeated again

1649 – Charles I executed after being accused of treason. Cromwell signs his death warrant
Cromwell leads an army to Ireland to restore order

1650 – Cromwell leaves Ireland and defeats the Scottish army who have declared their loyalty to the son of Charles I

1653 – Cromwell dissolves parliament and becomes Lord Protector

1658 – Cromwell dies
His son Richard becomes Lord Protector but steps down

1660 – King Charles II is restored to the throne

1661 – Cromwell's body is exhumed and hanged. He is beheaded.

1960 – Cromwell's head is reburied in a secret ceremony at Cambridge College

Acknowledgements

Many thanks to Paula Campbell in Poolbeg Press. I am very much indebted to you for the faith you have shown in me. Thanks also to Gaye Shortland, my editor, who has spent the last few years trying to knock me into shape. I very much appreciate the time and effort you have given to me and I hope I have become a more well-rounded writer as a result. Thanks also to everyone in Poolbeg Press who do such Trojan work for us – Kieran, Caroline, Dave, Lee, Orla, Andy, Ron and Conor. Thanks also to the very talented designer Derry Dillon whose illustrations have brought my various characters to life over the years.

I am very much obliged to Professor John Morrill for taking the time to answer a number of questions about Cromwell on a number of different occasions, and for providing me with some very insightful source material. Thanks also to Dr Jason McElligott who also provided material and Professor Ronald Hutton for permission to use his quote at the beginning of the book.

Thanks to Tony Dooley and Pat O'Brien for reviewing the drafts of this book and providing feedback. Thanks too to Nuala, Jean, Phil and Tom for providing those great dinners when they were most needed!

A word of thanks to everyone at Fingal Libraries, Children's Books Ireland, Writing.ie, Irish Writing Centre, Dublin Book Festival, Hays Festival, Tara Book Company, Canada Life Europe and the Irish Life Group who have always given me encouragement to follow my dream to write.

Thanks to John Manning in the *Fingal Independent* for those very complimentary articles about me over the years. I am in your debt! (John also wrote a very funny comedy sketch about Cromwell which I urge you to check out!)

A special word of thanks to Cyril Gillen, an inspirational English teacher, who encouraged a love of literature in me, and Brother Claude Hamill (R.I.P.) who introduced me to the wonders of history. To you, Brother Hamill, I say: I hope the readers "catch my drift" in this book.

A special mention to Jenny Mangan, Librarian, and the young people involved in the Creative Writing

Group at Larkin Community College in Dublin who continue to astound me with their enthusiasm and creativity every time I meet them. Keep writing! You could teach us all a thing or two!

Finally, a special thanks to Denise, Alex and Oisín for reviewing the drafts, and putting up with me for those long periods of time when all I could talk about was Cromwell, Cromwell, Cromwell! I could not do this without your support.

Books and Articles Referenced

This list is not exhaustive but provides a good representation of the books and articles referenced while researching the subject matter of this book.

Covington, Sarah. "'The Odious Demon from Across the Sea'. Oliver Cromwell, Memory and the Dislocations of Ireland" Kuijpers, E., Pollmann, J., Muller, J., van der Steen, J. (eds.) *Memory before Modernity – Practices of Memory in Early Modern Europe*. Brill, Leiden, The Netherlands, 2013.

Fraser, Antonia. *Cromwell, Our Chief of Men*. Weidenfeld and Nicolson. London, 1973.

Harrison, Frederic. *Oliver Cromwell*. Albion Press, 2016 (Originally pub. 1888)

Hume, David. *The History of England in Three Volumes, Vol. I Part E – From Charles I to Cromwell*. A Public Domain book. 1754–61.

Lenihan, Pádraig. *Confederate Catholics at War, 1641-49.* Cork University Press, 2000.

Morrill John. "The Religious Context of the Cromwellian Conquest of Ireland." Transactions of the Royal Historical Society, vol. 34, pp. 155–178, 1984.

Morrill John. "The Drogheda Massacre in Cromwellian Context" in Edwards, Lenihan, Tait (eds.) *Age of Atrocity: Violence and Political Conflict in Early Modern Ireland.* Four Courts Press, 2007.

Morrill John. "Cromwell, Parliament, Ireland and a Commonwealth in Crisis: 1652 Revisited". Parliamentary History, Vol. 30, pt. 2, pp. 193-214., 2011.

McElligott, Jason. "Cromwell, Drogheda and the abuse of Irish history." *Bullán: an Irish Studies Journal*, vi, no. 1 (Summer/Fall2001), 109-32.

Ó Sochrú, Micheál. *God's Executioner: Oliver Cromwell and the Conquest of Ireland.* Faber & Faber. 2008.

Reilly, Tom. *Cromwell was Framed – Ireland 1649.* Chronos Books, UK, 2014.

Shagan, Ethan Howard. "Constructing Discord: Ideology, Propaganda and English Responses to the Irish Rebellion of 1641." Journal of British Studies, Vol 36, No.1 pp 4-34. 1997.

Websites Referenced

BCW Project – Cromwell in Ireland
http://bcw-project.org/military/third-civil-war/cromwell-in-ireland/index

The Cromwell Association
http://www.olivercromwell.org/cromwelliana.htm

The Irish History Online Website – Some interesting articles on Cromwell and Tom Reilly
http://www.theirishstory.com/?s=cromwell#.WlPp5q5l-Uk

History Ireland
http://www.historyireland.com

Monty Python's Oliver Cromwell
Sing along to "Oliver Cromwell" with this official karaoke-style Monty Python lyric video
https://www.youtube.com/watch?v=dBPf6P332uM

As seen on the RTÉ Toy Show

Also available

The number one bestseller
30,000 copies sold

The Easter Rising 1916

Molly's Diary

Her own family is plunged into danger on both sides of the conflict. Her father, a technical officer with the Post Office dodges the crossfire as he tries to restore the telegraph lines while her wayward brother runs messages for the rebels. Molly, a trained First Aider, risks her own safety to help the wounded on both sides.

As violence and looting erupts in the streets of Dublin alongside heroism and high ideals, Molly records it all. The Proclamation at the GPO, the battle of Mount Street, the arrival of the British Troops. But will Molly's own family survive and will she be able to save her brother?

This is her diary.

ISBN 978-1-78199-9745

'Brilliantly imagined and gripping story from the heart of the 1916 Rising, based on meticulous research'
Joe Duffy, broadcaster and author of *Children of the Rising*

Patricia Murphy

Also available

The War of Independence 1920-22

Dan's Diary

It's 1920 and as the War of Independence rages in Ireland, ace schoolboy footballer Dan becomes a trusted messenger for rebel leader Michael Collins. But, despite a promise to his cousin Molly to never fire a gun, he is pulled deeper into the struggle.

Dan's activities draw the attention of a sinister British spy and he and Molly are forced to flee Dublin. On the run, they meet Flying Columns and as Cork burns narrowly escape death.

But unknown to Dan, he holds the key to an evil plot to derail any chance for peace. And his enemy will stop at nothing to track him down.

Will Dan and Molly save the day and can the leaders bring peace to Ireland?

ISBN 978-1-78199-8410

Patricia Murphy

Also available

The Irish Civil War 1922-23

Ava's Diary

Life sucks for twelve-year-old Irish-American Ava when she is dragged back to Dublin by her mother after her parents' messy divorce. She is bullied at her new school and her only friend is moody teenage neighbour Mal, who has secrets of his own.

But when Ava finds a sliver of an emerald and a bundle of old letters in the attic, she is plunged into a historical mystery linking the missing crown jewels of Tsarist Russia to the heart of Ireland's bloody civil war in 1922.

As a newly independent Ireland split over supporting the new Free State or fighting on for a Republic, danger lurked around every corner and friends became foes. Who was the author of the letters, young medical student Molly O'Donovan? Why did her brother Jack the Cat smuggle the jewels from the United States and end up on the run from both sides? And did her football mad cousin Dan survive running messages through the crossfire?

Through the eyes of Molly, Ava encounters the death of Michael Collins, deadly ambushes in Kerry and the tragic fate of former comrades.

As Ava learns about the bitter civil war, she is forced to confront the conflict in her own life. Can the journey into the past help her to learn the importance of reconciliation and new beginnings?

ISBN 978-1-78199-8823

Patricia Murphy

Also available

Three Battles for Independence

Seeds of Liberty

Three countries – three revolutions – three children caught
up in the struggle for freedom.

Boston 1770s
All Jack wants is to stay out of trouble – but when the fighting
breaks out, he knows he'll need to pick a side.

Paris 1790s
Catherine is thrilled by the Revolution and the promise of a
better future for all. But terror will soon take over the city.

Wexford 1798
Robert's brothers tell him he's too young to take part
in the Rising, but he's determined to prove them wrong.

Liberty can be won – but there's always a price to be paid.

ISBN 978-1-78199-9738

Claire Hennessy

If you enjoyed this book from
Poolbeg why not visit our website

www.poolbeg.com

and get another book delivered straight
to your home or to a friend's home?

All books despatched within 24 hours.

Free postage on orders over €25*

Why not join our mailing list at
www.poolbeg.com and get some
fantastic offers, competitions,
author interviews, new releases
and much more?

@PoolbegBooks

www.facebook.com/poolbegpress

*Free postage over €25 applies to Ireland only